T0128899

THE OTHER SIDE
OF MOTOWN

THE OTHER SIDE OF MOTOWN

Audrey Thorpe

THE OTHER SIDE OF MOTOWN

iUniverse books may be ordered through booksellers or by contacting:

iUniverse
1663 Liberty Drive
Bloomington, IN 47403
www.iuniverse.com
1-800-Authors (1-800-288-4677)

ISBN: 978-1-5320-7325-0 (sc)
ISBN: 978-1-5320-7326-7 (e)

Library of Congress Control Number: 2019904501

Print information available on the last page.

iUniverse rev. date: 04/23/2019

To my beloved cousins, Dr. Clarita Hughes and Gwendolyn Crooks, and my lifelong friends, for their love, trust, encouragement, and inspiration: Myrna Webb, Gloria Davis, Lois Banks, Margarie Lamb, Sonya Harris, and Marilyn Madlinger.

CHAPTER 1

It was early autumn in 1965 when Maria Arlington began working for Motown Record Corporation. Motown was in its heyday, producing number one hit records that were being sold worldwide. The record company's offices on West Grand Boulevard in Detroit, Michigan, were located in eight buildings that had once been spacious brick houses but were now converted into offices. One of the buildings housed Jobete Music, which was a division of Motown that contained all its copyrighted music.

Maria began working in the Department of International Talent Management, which was located two doors over from the main office that was named "Hitsville, USA." The recording studio was also at the Hitsville site.

Maria had completed a two-year business-training program at a local community college and began working as an assistant to a talent manager who handled the business affairs for five Motown artists. She was nineteen years of age and greatly enjoyed her exciting job.

Every week, she assisted the talent manager in scheduling concert dates for the artists; she would record the dates and the price of the concerts in a large ledger. She would also schedule travel for the artists and hotel accommodations and prepare travel itineraries for them.

In addition to taking care of the artists' appearances, nationally and internationally, she also assisted the talent manager by preparing letters to booking agents, to managers of various entertainment centers, and to media executives. Whenever the talent manager traveled to major cities to meet television hosts or managers of concert halls, she would travel with her, to assist her in making these contacts. Maria also attended monthly administrative staff meetings with the talent manager, and she took notes that she later transcribed into minutes.

Often when she was at the Hitsville office to attend meetings, she saw Greg Richmond, a trumpeter who played with the musicians in recording background music for the artists. She developed a crush on the handsome, well-built trumpeter, who simply blew her away with his casual sexiness and dynamic talent.

By March 1969, after having worked for Motown for three and a half years, the excitement of being around so many well-known artists and a strong team of producers, songwriters, musicians, and arrangers had worn off. Maria knew she had to establish a career for herself. She had read many great classical novels and was an A student in English literature. Now she had a burning desire to become a writer and decided she'd apply to work at Wayne State University and attend evening classes there. She did not want to apply for any student loans, which she felt would be cumbersome to repay. Rather, she would enroll in English classes and pay for them each semester. Eventually, she would also take history classes. She felt she could manage her expenses that way and earn an associate's degree. Her goal was to become a novelist, and she felt her classes would help her to develop writing skills.

Maria resigned from Motown and applied for work at Wayne State. After she took a battery of tests, a personnel manager at the university contacted her and offered her a position as an admissions officer in the Graduate School of Social Work. She accepted the position and quickly went to work at the school, processing applications for admission. The work required great diligence in carefully keeping records of more than three hundred students and computing weekly and monthly statistical admission reports. Some graduate schools had at least three people who took care of the admissions process, but Maria was the only admissions officer for the Graduate School of Social Work.

While working at Wayne State and taking part-time classes, she often thought about Greg Richmond, the trumpeter she'd had a crush on at Motown. Her friends couldn't get over how she deeply admired a band member, rather than one of the exciting singers like Marvin Gaye or Smokey, but Maria was struck by Greg's sharp intelligence and finesse, and she loved his stance as he pumped away on his trumpet. His maturity and brilliance ignited her with passion; however, in a few years, Greg left Detroit.

CHAPTER 2

When Motown moved to California in 1972, Greg moved with them. Maria never saw him again. She heard through the grapevine that he and his wife owned a lovely home in LA and his wife had given birth to twin boys. She regretted that she never had a chance to get to know him, but she was glad to know he was doing well.

By 1972, Maria had been living alone in an apartment near Wayne State for four years and had not been dating until one day in the fall of '72. David Silverman noticed her in a campus restaurant and decided to join her for lunch. He was a history professor, thirty-six years of age, and single, somewhat of a loner like Maria. He walked up to her and introduced himself, and she agreed to have lunch with him. She enjoyed conversing with him. History was one of her favorite subjects, and she was glad David was willing to help her with some of her many questions about the First World War. He enjoyed her enthusiasm about a subject he had been teaching for many years. They regularly met for lunch for three months and then advanced to having dinner together. He was a shy Jewish man, tall and lanky, with smooth olive skin and a shock of black hair. He had a strong nose and small, private eyes that seemed to hide behind a pair of wire-framed eyeglasses. He was reserved but pleasant, and Maria would often peer into his eyes to try to evaluate his mood.

Through their conversations, she learned that he had been engaged once to a white lady whom his dominant mother disapproved of him dating, and he had been hurt by her critical remarks about her. He related that his mother called his fiancée "white trash" and criticized her for chain-smoking and for her "harsh" laughter. Just the sight of her irritated his mother. She also disliked the fact that his fiancée managed a trailer park, which she strongly condemned, informing David that her work was beneath the dignity of their family. His mother insulted and humiliated his fiancée to the point that she broke off their engagement.

He had lived with his widowed mother until only two years ago, when he was thirty-four years old. He said he stayed with her to help her at home, but he was quite relieved when he moved out. He was now living in an apartment in Sherwood Forest, not too far from the university.

His hands always trembled, which Maria keenly observed. He told Maria that one day when he was sixteen, he accidentally dropped a bucket of paint on the front porch of his parents' home and his father went into such a rage he feared his father would kill him. He said his father called him a stupid son of a bitch and that he felt like cutting his hands off. He said that since that day, he could never keep his hands from shaking.

Maria felt that both of his parents had been insane, and she wondered why they had been so cruel to David, their only son, who was very meek. She had lost her parents when she was fifteen. They were killed in a car accident, and she began living with her grandparents until she enrolled in business college. She was also an only child, but her grandparents and her parents had been very loving people.

She felt sorry for David, who seemed to have missed out on love, not only from his parents but from a girlfriend as well. He told Maria that he was in love when he was twenty-one years old but that his girlfriend's parents moved them to Boston and he never saw her again.

Maria had dated in high school, but after her boyfriend joined the army, she lost contact with him. Once he completed his military obligation, he moved to another state.

CHAPTER 3

Maria was drawn to David because he was very kind and humble, and she realized how much he was attracted to her. She had never dated someone of a different race. She had only known men of her own race, African American, but she had such great esteem for David and his career as a history professor that his race became unimportant to her.

One evening when she was dining with him, she finally took the courage to confront him about her race. "David," she said, "if your mother disapproved of that white lady you became engaged to, how will she react to me?"

She remembered how his hands shook even more after she posed that question.

"Well," he said as he fumbled with his food while they dined in a restaurant, "now she's mostly senile."

Maria really laughed, and suddenly she noticed how steady his hands became as he stared at her. She felt it was a miracle how steady his hands had become.

Maria has been such a good friend to me, he thought as he stared at her. *She has accepted everything about me—my insecurities as well as my strengths. She has also disregarded how bitter and cruel my mother can be and has never let anything interfere in our dating.* He was greatly attracted to her, and he could feel his confidence returning, even though his parents had done much to destroy it. He and Maria continued to dine, and his hands remained calm throughout the evening.

A year later, he put his mother into an assisted living facility, sold her home, and bought himself a handsome house in Sherwood Forest. Then he married Maria. Two years later, they had a son whom they named Jonathan David Silverman. His old mother was always very excited to see her grandson whenever David and Maria visited her at the facility. David had never seen his mother so happy. She loved holding Jonathan, which seemed to have changed her entire life.

David and Maria were glad their son brought his mother so much joy. David never imagined he'd ever see his mother happy in life. He knew his parents had become extremely bitter after they were forced to give up their furniture business in Germany and flee the country during Hitler's regime. They lived in poverty in Amsterdam for several years before they were able to travel to America. They arrived in America in the late 1940s, and eventually they were able to reestablish their furniture business.

David's mother was able to enjoy her grandson until he was three years of age, before she passed away. David mourned the loss of his mother, but parenting his son gave him so much joy. He and Maria loved and cherished every moment of raising Jonathan. He had light-brown skin and silky black hair like his mother, along with his father's strong nose and small eyes. He was growing up very quickly, developing into a tall and limber young boy like his father.

During Jonathan's teen years, he and David enjoyed hiking, swimming, canoeing, and camping together. Maria sometimes joined them in outdoor activities, but she was mostly active in her Baptist church and in writing novels at home. She and Jonathan would also attend the Jewish temple with David, which he had been attending all his life.

Maria had obtained a bachelor's degree in English and history at Wayne State, and she had completed four novels. She would choose her best novel to submit to a publisher and pray for acceptance. She knew it was quite difficult for a new writer to become accepted by a large publishing company, but she would carefully select a publisher that would be interested in stories about individuals and families and their struggles to maintain their health, employment, and adequate standards of living. Most of all, Maria's stories emphasized the need for love in a loveless world. She knew love was necessary in order to remain balanced in life and to have good relations with others.

CHAPTER 4

David enjoyed taking Jonathan to hockey and basketball games, and he'd spend time discussing his future plans for college. Jonathan expressed to his father that he wanted to attend UCLA and study marine life—how to protect our vast waters and the variety of marine life that was being destroyed by oil and chemical spills. David told him that after he obtained his degree, he could work for an environmental company almost anywhere in the world. Jonathan was excited about starting his career in helping to protect the environment and was reading all he could about the earth.

In a short while, he received his acceptance letter from the University of California at Los Angeles, approving him for admission in the fall. He informed his parents, and they congratulated him. His father scheduled his flight to California, and in two weeks, he and Maria drove him to the airport. David and Maria hugged Jonathan tightly, as if he were heading to China. They had watery eyes and heavy hearts, realizing how much they would miss him. They had been a very close family. They waved goodbye as he boarded the plane, and their hearts sank deep within their chests as they reflected on how their lives had been centered around their only child.

Back at home, David and Maria hugged and kissed for a while. They knew they would greatly miss Jonathan, but they both had careers at the university that would keep them busy, and they enjoyed meeting each other at least once a month on campus for lunch.

Maria had been promoted to the position of admissions and orientation supervisor. She was no longer processing applications for admission to the Graduate School of Social Work; instead she was supervising admission clerks, and she planned orientations for new students that would help them to become familiar with the school.

David often took his history students on class trips to historic sites in the United States. Maria had adjusted to his absence from home at least three or four times a year as he traveled with his students. He took them to the Capitol in Washington, the Alamo in Texas, to Arlington Cemetery in Virginia, and to view the Liberty Bell in Philadelphia. David loved these trips, which helped to bring history to life for his students.

Maria remembered how David told her that while he was in his first year of college at Eastern Michigan University, he played Abraham Lincoln in a play called *The Price of Freedom*. David related to her that everyone felt he looked so much like President Lincoln that they often teased him by saying, "Hey, Abe, how's it going?"

Maria imagined that he would have looked almost identical to President Lincoln, being so tall and lanky and having a shock of black hair. Once he added a beard and old-fashioned eyeglasses, he was like a living legend.

Whenever David was away from home, she would write hundreds of pages in her novel about an American family in the twentieth or twenty-first century and how they were able to survive social and economic changes. Being able to survive while under adversities and hardships was always one of Maria's main concerns. She realized that many Americans would strive hard to achieve success—the American Dream—but she was also painfully aware of the social unrest and the economic decline that was sweeping across the nation. Her stories focused on individuals and families being able to endure unexpected challenges.

When David returned home from a trip, they made love and dined together at home. They both loved to cook, and sometimes they would call Jonathan and turn on the speaker so that they could both listen to him and talk.

CHAPTER 5

During Jonathan's second year in college in 1994, he came home during the summer break and enjoyed many activities with his parents. They went on picnics and to baseball games and took scenic drives through Canada. Most of all, they loved dining at home together and listening to Jonathan's conversations about the environment and about some of the students he had met on UCLA's campus.

At the end of Jonathan's visit, Maria desired to travel with him to California so she could visit where he lived on campus, in a house with four other male students. She wanted to make sure he was in good company. David had too many responsibilities at the university, in preparing exams and lectures, so he was unable to travel with them. He told Jonathan that he and Maria would visit him for two weeks prior to graduation, and Jonathan was happy to know that.

The flight to LA was smooth and relaxing, and Maria enjoyed every moment of it. Jonathan was anxious to show her around UCLA's campus. She had booked a room at the Marriott, which was only fifteen minutes from campus, and that made it easy for her to be able to visit Jonathan.

Once the plane landed in Los Angeles, Jonathan and Maria recovered their luggage and boarded a bus to UCLA. Exhausted upon their arrival at the university, Maria spotted a cab and quickly hailed it. She gave Jonathan a brisk kiss on the cheek and told him she'd call him the next afternoon. He told her that would be fine, and she scurried away.

That next day, Maria took a cab to Jonathan's home, which was close to campus, and Jonathan answered the door when she rang the bell. There were smiles and hugs, and Jonathan invited his mother in and introduced her to two of his roommates. Maria was pleased to meet them. The house was quite large, with two bedrooms on the first floor and two on the second. Maria was surprised to see how neat and clean the home was.

"One of our roommates, Steven Gasielle, is slightly older than us. He spent three years in the army before coming here to school, and he acts like a dorm captain. He insists on neatness and cleanliness," Jonathan explained.

Maria laughed. "It's a good thing you have him. He'll keep you on your toes."

"Yeah, it really is good that he's here." Jonathan grinned. "Because Brad Johnson and Rick Carter are so lazy. One day Brad was in the living room, and he peeled a banana and threw the peel on the cocktail table, and Steven sprung on him with this big, long ruler and slapped his hands. Boy, Brad rolled his eyes at Steven, and I know he wanted to fight him, but Steven's good in karate, and so Brad had to sit quietly for a while, and then he got up and removed the banana peel from the table and threw it in the trash."

Maria's face glowed as Jonathan related the incident. "Well, it's good your home is kept clean," she said.

"Yeah, it really is."

They had toured the house while Rick Carter and Charles Tatum, Jonathan's roommates, were slouched on the sofa, drinking sodas, and watching *Let's Make a Deal* on television.

"Is there a restaurant close by?" Maria asked.

"Yeah, Mexican Gardens. It's just three blocks from here. We can go there. Bye, guys," Jonathan said.

"Goodbye. It was nice meeting you, Mrs. Silverman," they said.

"Thank you. It was nice meeting you also."

CHAPTER 6

Jonathan and Maria walked into the bright sunlight and heat. It was late summer, but unlike Michigan, the heat lasted much longer here. They took a leisurely walk to the Mexican restaurant, and Maria enjoyed viewing all the stucco homes in the area and the variety of plants in the front lawns. You'd never see plants in anyone's front lawn in Michigan; only green grass, but Californians had altogether different views of landscape. Many fences were covered in vines with floral blossoms, and occasionally a palm tree popped up out of nowhere. Maria felt humored by the landscape.

Soon, they were inside the restaurant, and a friendly Mexican lady quickly took their food orders.

"I've met a girl," Jonathan told his mother.

Maria blushed. Her son was now nineteen years old, and very tall and handsome. He had thick curly hair and strong features like his father. She was sure he had probably met several girls.

"What's her name?"

"Nicole Kenika."

"Kenika?" Maria looked slightly baffled.

Jonathan grinned. "She's Hawaiian."

"Oh, I see." Maria quickly wondered if Miss Nicole Kenika was luring her son away from his studies. "Does she live on campus?"

"Yes, she's in a dorm. She's a very sweet lady, about five-seven, medium size, and has very long, black wavy hair. We have an environmental science class together."

Just then, the waitress walked up and sat down their botanas and lemonade. They began eating.

"So, she plans to become an environmentalist also?"

"Yeah, and we plan to marry after we graduate and work together in her hometown in Honolulu."

"Whoa, wait a minute!" Maria laughed. "You mean you're thinking that far ahead? And you're willing to move all the way to Hawaii and forsake me and your dad?"

"You and Dad will retire one day, and you can visit us in Hawaii."

"Jonathan, really, David and I might not retire for at least another ten or twelve years."

"So, you can still visit us. Time passes very quickly. I'll soon start my second year in college. Don't worry about time. You and Dad can always vacation in Hawaii."

Maria felt water filling her eyes.

"Yes, that's true, David and I can always visit you in Hawaii, but I hope you know that's not the same as having you back home." Maria wiped away the water in her eyes. "I don't mean back at home with us, but being back in Michigan."

"Location is not a big deal anymore, Mother. People travel all the time these days. Besides, you should be willing to explore other parts of the world. You can't just huddle in your bedroom and write forever. You need to see more of the world."

Maria stared at Jonathan for a long while, trying to decide whether he was being encouraging or sinister. She had to take the middle road and quickly decided it was up to her how she would feel about him living so far away. They slowly ate and were quiet for a few minutes. Finally, Maria continued their conversation.

"Jonathan, I love being in my room at home, writing novels. It allows me an opportunity to open up and express my views about life, about the things I feel are most important in life. I write about how we must be willing to accept change, but I never thought for a moment that you would tell me that you plan to live in Hawaii. And if Nicole means that much to you, why didn't you invite her to dinner with us?"

"Because she's in Hawaii."

Jonathan's answer forced a smile on Maria's face. Her son had hit her hard with very surprising news, but she was glad that he was happy and doing well in school.

After dinner, Maria and Jonathan walked around UCLA's campus, and Jonathan told her about several buildings there. They went inside the main library, which Jonathan knew his mother would enjoy.

CHAPTER 7

Maria spent six days with Jonathan and loved every minute of it. He borrowed a roommate's car and drove her all around the vast city of Los Angeles. Maria quickly decided that she wouldn't care to live there because there was too much traffic congestion, and she didn't like seeing all the different gangs in certain areas of the city. Jonathan drove through Hollywood, which Maria felt was bizarre, but she enjoyed collecting souvenirs from there. Jonathan drove her through the plush city of Beverly Hills, and Maria couldn't imagine how much money it took to live there. Jonathan constantly talked about Nicole and how anxious he was for her to return home from Hawaii. He also talked about how he loved the great beaches in California.

Soon, Maria's visit came to an end, and Jonathan drove her to the airport. She checked her baggage, and they headed to gate C22 to wait for an American Airlines flight to Detroit that would depart at 1:40 p.m.

While they were sitting at gate C22, Maria heard a voice say, "Maria Arlington?"

Maria looked up, and there stood Greg Richmond, the trumpeter who had played in Motown's band. She couldn't believe her eyes.

"It's Maria Silverman," she replied, smiling, "and this is my son, Jonathan."

"It's good to see you, Maria, and it's nice meeting you, Jonathan."

"It's good to meet you also," Jonathan said.

Greg shook their hands. Maria felt Greg hadn't changed much at all over the years. He was nearly the same size as when they worked at Motown. He was five-feet-ten and weighed about 150 pounds.

"What brought you to LA?" Greg asked.

"My son is a student at UCLA. I came to visit him."

"I'm glad I've had a chance to see you. I have my own band now—Greg Richmond and the Soul Invaders. We came together a few years after Berry sold Motown."

"Wow! You worked for Motown!" Jonathan exclaimed. "My mother told me a lot about Motown while I was growing up. I love the Temptations."

"Those were truly the good old days, when your mother and I worked at Motown." Greg smiled. "Maria, it's been very nice talking with you and Jonathan, but I have to rush to catch my plane. I'm heading to New Orleans, where my band will be performing in a music festival."

"Do you still live here in LA?" Maria asked.

"Yes. You can contact me anytime you'd like at the Greg Richmond Music Company here in LA."

"Okay, thanks for letting me know."

"Take care," Greg said as he rushed away.

"Wow, what an inspirited person," Jonathan commented.

Maria sighed. *All those years at Motown,* she thought, *and Greg and I never spent much time together.* She dismissed her thoughts.

"Yes, he does have a lot of energy, Jonathan," she said, "but musicians are like that."

In a short while, it was time for Maria to board her plane, and she and Jonathan hugged before she scurried away.

CHAPTER 8

Later that year, on Thanksgiving Day, David and Maria had dinner at David's aunt Sybil and uncle Isaac's home. They had moved to Birmingham, Michigan, after having lived on Detroit's northwest side for forty-five years.

David and Maria spent nearly three hours talking with David's aunt and uncle about the history of Detroit. They had been able to escape Germany and come to America in the early forties. They felt passionate about American life and protective of the deep roots they had cultivated in American culture. They hated leaving their spacious home in northwest Detroit, but they avoided commenting on how the African American population had become too much of a threat to them. They respected David's marriage to Maria and didn't want to hurt their feelings in any way, but they found that many young African Americans had become wild and confrontational, and they were forced to move. They did not dislike African Americans. They had objected to David's mother's criticisms about Maria. They were very fond of David and Maria, and they were also pleasant toward many African Americans who had worked just as hard in life as they had, but the young ones needed discipline.

The day after Thanksgiving, David took Maria on a weekend trip to the small city of Frankenmuth, a tourist city north of Detroit.

While David drove north on I-75, he thought about how many of his relatives had passed away, but fortunately, his mother's sister and her husband were still alive.

"Aunt Sybil and Uncle Isaac are so elderly," David commented. "It's a wonder they haven't hired servants and caregivers. They have millions stored up. Uncle Isaac owned insurance companies in Detroit and in the Midwest."

"How old are they?" Maria inquired.

"Aunt Sybil is eighty-four, and Uncle Isaac is eighty-seven."

"They seem to be doing well."

"On the surface," David answered. "Arthur Rosenberg, who used to work for Uncle Isaac at one of his insurance companies in Detroit, called me a few days ago and told me he had been to visit Uncle Isaac, and that his garage door was open and that there was mail in his mailbox that had been there for weeks. He closed his garage door, and he took him his mail."

"So, he and your aunt are very forgetful."

"Yes, and that's not good. I'm going to call the Jewish Welfare Agency and ask them to send a social worker to visit with them. They need help. They should have a caregiver."

"Yes, well, you should call the agency, David."

"I will." David drove steadily north. "I've booked us a room at the Comfort Inn, so that after we've dined and toured the shopping area, we won't have to rush back home."

"That was a good idea," Maria said. "I'm glad you won't have to drive home in the dark on a cold winter night."

They arrived in Frankenmuth close to noon and checked into the Comfort Inn. By one thirty, they were having lunch at the Bavarian, a banquet restaurant, where they dined with nearly one hundred people. They enjoyed meeting people from several different cities. While dining, a country music group known as the Clovers sang eight of their songs. Maria enjoyed their strong, melodious voices and the good music. Four musicians accommodated them. Two hours later, the pair began walking through the shopping area.

After touring the commercial district in Frankenmuth, they retreated to their hotel room. They felt as if they were on a small, private second honeymoon. They needed this weekend together. David knew that this trip was one of the ways he could keep their lovemaking exciting and keep their lives vibrant, especially since Jonathan was no longer with them. While they were dressing for bed, Maria told David all about Jonathan's female friend, and David said he was happy for him.

They enjoyed the warmth in their cozy motel room. Outside, cold winds were blowing, and snowflakes were twirling in the rigid air, but inside, they cuddled and kissed and enjoyed tender lovemaking until they were sound asleep.

CHAPTER 9

The years quickly passed, and soon it was 1997, and David and Maria were in Los Angeles, staying at the Sheraton Hotel for two weeks. They arrived a week before Jonathan's graduation from UCLA, and Jonathan and his fiancée, Nicole, took them sightseeing and to a Hugh Masekela concert at an outdoor concert theater. Hugh Masekela's beautiful jazz music, stemming from his African origin, was flourishing across the world, and *Grazing in the Grass* was one of his most enduring records.

The following week, they were at Jonathan's graduation ceremony in an auditorium on campus. They joyfully watched Jonathan and Nicole accept their diplomas, and Maria snapped several pictures of them. After the ceremony, they dined together inside the Sheraton, and Nicole talked about how she grew up in Hawaii and had learned three languages while living there. Jonathan expressed how anxious he was to live in Hawaii and how he couldn't wait to leave for the island in August. He and Nicole would get married the following year.

"And you both have been accepted to work for the Department of Natural Resources on the island?" David commented while they dined. Nicole and Jonathan were having lamb shank and rice, and David and Maria were enjoying filet mignon with red skins.

"Yes, we'll both work for the department beginning on September 15," Jonathan replied.

"We had phone interviews," Nicole informed David and Maria. "We'll start working in water conservation, conducting regular inspections, and eventually we plan to seek managerial positions."

"You have excellent goals," Maria said.

"Thanks, Mother," Jonathan replied. "And we're going to do a lot of scuba diving."

"That sounds like you," Maria said. "Nicole, don't let him venture too far into the unknown. He's always loved adventure, but make sure he sets limits."

"Oh, I will," Nicole responded. "I'm not a fish!" She laughed.

"But she is an excellent swimmer," Jonathan added.

"So, Jonathan, you plan to rent a room in the home of a family that has lived on the island for over twenty years?" David inquired.

"Yes, the home of Mr. and Mrs. Biel. They own a restaurant on the island, Biel's Seafood Grill. They are from New Orleans. They have a son who joined the navy two years ago and plans to remain in the navy until he retires, so the Biels rent to college students and others who are new to the island. They never rent to more than two people at once, and you must agree to rent by the year."

"How much rent will you pay?" Maria asked.

"Five hundred dollars a month, utilities included. The medical student, a guy from Chicago, who will also be renting a room while I'm there, will pay the same amount," Jonathan said.

"And Nicole, you're going to live with your parents?" David asked.

"Yes, that's right. My father, Samuel Kenika, is an auto mechanic at a Toyota dealership, and my mother, Kyleena, is a yoga instructor. My sister, Serena, who is nineteen, lives at home. She's studying choreography at a local junior college. She wants to work on Broadway."

"You have a nice family." Maria smiled.

"Thank you. My mother and my sister will help me plan my wedding next year. Jonathan and I will get married at a chapel."

"And, of course, David and I will attend your wedding," Maria said. "You and Jonathan can pick a reasonable hotel for us on the island where we can stay for ten days. We're working people, and we can't stay away too long from our jobs at the university."

"I understand," Nicole said. "Jonathan and I will find a nice hotel for you."

After a few days, David and Maria boarded a plane and were on their way back to Detroit. They were immensely happy that Jonathan had graduated from UCLA and that he had found a lovely, sweet girlfriend whom he planned to marry.

CHAPTER 10

Once at home in Sherwood Forest, David was happy that the grass had been cut. Their lawn care man, Tony Collins, was a young father who was doing all he could to support his family and was very faithful in caring for their lawns.

David retrieved the mail from the mailbox, went into the dining room, sat down, and looked over all the bills. Maria was down the hall in the master bedroom, putting away her clothes from her suitcases. Their four-bedroom colonial home was very quiet. David wondered if he and Maria had made a mistake by having only one child, but he quickly reminded himself about how hard he worked at the university and how he was always surrounded by many students. His students were like a family to him.

Maria appeared next to him. "I really like Nicole," she said as she sat.

"So do I," he replied, glancing at the property tax bill. The taxes were always outrageously high, as if they were being charged nearly half of the expenses to maintain Detroit. David felt that the wealthy citizens in his neighborhood were being targeted to pay more than their fair share in property taxes. He knew it was time to speak up about the taxes at one of their block club meetings. The gas bills were astronomical in the winter, even when he lowered the thermostat while he and Maria were away at work.

"I miss Jonathan," Maria said, feeling the sharp reality of how she and David were empty-nesters.

David gazed into space, realizing the entire house was quiet. He immediately experienced a flashback, envisioning Jonathan in his upstairs bedroom, listening to rap music as he read, and how he always questioned him about "those awful lyrics in the music." Jonathan told him that the lyrics were about the real world and everyday life.

"The real world?" David would say to him. "Where people haven't any respect for anything?"

He could see Jonathan gazing at him innocently. He always wished his son would listen to Michael Jackson or Prince or to any of the Motown artists. His blood pressure went up every time he heard a rapper spewing out hate or anger, but his son felt it was "artistic expression."

"I know I annoyed him quite a bit," David said. "I always wanted him to get rid of his rap music."

"I thought it was sort of fun," Maria said, "although I couldn't understand half of it, as fast as those rappers spit out words. I knew Jonathan was concerned about how his peers felt, and so I was okay with that. He sampled Motown's music for a while and then settled for rap."

Now the house was too quiet for her.

"His peers were full of hate," David grumbled, "which should have been obvious to him. There were times I insisted he cut that music off."

David gathered his bills and said he needed to go unpack. He headed down the hallway to the bedroom, and Maria went into the kitchen and began preparing their dinner.

CHAPTER 11

Near the end of summer, Tony rang the doorbell after he finished cutting the grass and sweeping the sidewalk and driveway. He had been helping the Silvermans for many years, but his work on their lawns was ending today.

David answered the door. "Hello, Tony."

"Hello, Mr. Silverman. Today is my last day of work here."

"Oh?" David looked surprised. "Well, let me pay you." He took out his wallet, grabbed thirty-five dollars, and handed it to Tony. "I wasn't aware that you were quitting today."

"Neither was I," Tony said, "but a lawyer in Tennessee called me. My uncle died, and he willed me his home. It's a three-bedroom ranch. He and his wife didn't have any children, and his wife died five years ago, so I will be moving into his home."

Tony was thirty years old and African American. He had been working three jobs for several years in order to care for his wife and three children. He had been employed as a delivery truck driver for a furniture company until the company went out of business.

"What city will you be living in in Tennessee?" David inquired.

"Memphis," Tony replied. "My uncle's home is paid for, and there are plenty of jobs in Memphis. I'm sure I can return to work at a furniture company."

"You shouldn't have a problem finding work. You are an excellent worker, and they manufacture a lot of furniture in the South. My parents once owned a furniture store."

"Thanks for your encouragement, Mr. Silverman. I appreciate it. Give Mrs. Silverman my regards."

"I will."

Tony walked away, and David closed the door.

Maria was in the kitchen preparing breakfast. David went into the kitchen, poured himself a cup of coffee, and sat at the kitchen table.

"Was that Tony at the door?" Maria asked.

"Yes," David said. "He just quit working for us."

"Oh, for heaven's sake," Maria moaned. "We'll never find another lawn-care man as dependable as Tony."

She poured pancake mix into a large skillet with hot cooking oil.

"Well, you know that guy who used to work for Motown? You said he was a chauffeur for the Gordy family and Stevie Wonder, but now he owns a nursery. Ask him if he can recommend a lawn-care guy," David suggested.

"Oh, you're right!" Maria said excitedly as she flipped pancakes. "Lenny Jackson! You're so right! He opened a large nursery on Eight Mile Road a few years ago, and I went there and bought quite a few plants from him. I'll drive by there today after we have breakfast. I'm sure he can recommend someone."

"It will be good to know who we have helping us around our home," David said.

"You're absolutely right," Maria replied.

CHAPTER 12

An hour later, Maria drove to the LJ Nursery on Eight Mile Road. "LJ" stood for Lenny Jackson. As she pulled into the parking lot, she saw Lenny helping a delivery man to unload potted flowers near the entrance to the nursery. She quickly parked her Mazda, got out, and rushed toward Lenny.

"Lenny!" she called out.

Lenny set down a pot of geraniums. He was medium height, very slender, with a dark-chocolate complexion and tightly curled black hair. He was one of the nicest persons Maria had ever known.

"Maria, I haven't seen you in a lot of years!" Lenny smiled, and they hugged. "So, how is everything?"

"Real fine. My husband and I went to California a few months ago to see our son graduate from UCLA."

"That's good. Did you visit anyone from Motown?"

"No, but I ran into Greg Richmond at the airport."

"He still playing that trumpet?" Lenny said.

"Yes, he is. Lenny, I need someone to cut my grass. Our lawn-care guy just quit. Can you recommend someone?"

"Sure. Me."

Maria looked baffled. "But you have to work here at your nursery."

"My brother, Andrew, is in charge of this nursery. He lost his job at Ford Motor, so I gave this job to him. I'd rather freelance as a landscaper. I love to move about; that's why I was a driver at Motown.

I don't like to be confined, but I come here for a few hours each week and help out."

"Lenny, are you sure you wouldn't mind taking care of our lawns? You have a lot of responsibility on your hands."

Lenny took a pen and a small notebook from his shirt pocket. "Here, give me your address and phone number. I'll come by your house every two weeks and cut your grass. I'll get there between six and seven in the morning before I start my workday."

Maria wrote down her name, address, and phone number and handed it to Lenny.

"Oh, so you're on Somerset Drive."

"Yes, between Six and Seven Mile Road."

"I know where you are. You're in Sherwood Forest. I've done a lot of landscape work in your neighborhood."

"How much do you charge for lawn care?"

"A cup of coffee would be fine, Maria."

"Lenny, that's ridiculous!"

"Okay, so you can add sausage and toast."

"My husband would find that very odd."

"So, just give me a large coffee in a Styrofoam cup, and that would be good. I give everyone who used to work at Motown a discount."

"Lenny," Maria said, "a cup of coffee is not a discount; that's free service! I'll give you the coffee and a tip."

"Okay, if you insist. I'll start cutting your grass a week from today. I have to go now and help that delivery driver. I'll talk with you later."

Lenny rushed back to the delivery truck, and Maria went to her car, got in, and drove away.

There were only a few weeks of summer remaining that year, and Lenny came to the Silvermans' home every two weeks and cut their grass. One Saturday morning, he arrived a half hour after David had taken his Buick to the car dealership for service. Maria invited him into her home for breakfast.

CHAPTER 13

They sat in the kitchen and ate scrambled eggs, canadian bacon, and toast and drank coffee. "Lenny, so many singers who worked for Motown have passed away," Maria said.

"Yes, I know. It seems that after Tammi Terrell and Paul Williams of the Temptations died, several other artists died a tragic death."

"Especially David Ruffin and Marvin Gaye," Maria said.

"And Florence Ballard who wasted her youthful life arguing about who should lead the Supremes."

"And, others died from illnesses, such as Eddie Kendricks and Melvin Franklin, who were in the Temptations," Maria sadly recounted.

"Yes, and Obie Benson and Lawrence Payton of the Four Tops passed away. And before Motown moved to California in '72, several artists had quit working for them, but I went out there along with Berry and his family, Diana Ross, Smokey Robinson, Stevie Wonder, the Temptations, and Marvin Gaye."

"And Motown signed on many new artists while they were in California," Maria commented. "They had Michael Jackson and the Jackson Five, DeBarge, Teena Marie, Lionel Richie, Rick James, and other artists."

"Yeah, that's true. Other record companies had snatched many of Motown's artists. RCA offered Diana Ross one of the largest record contracts in music history for twenty million dollars," Lenny said while he and Maria finished their breakfast.

"But you kept chauffeuring for Berry and the Gordy family and Stevie Wonder while you were in California."

"That's right. My wife, Shirley, and my children relocated with me to California. We had a small home, and our two children finished high school in Los Angeles. We were out there from 1972 until 1990, and then we returned home."

"So, how is Shirley?"

"She's okay. We separated last year. She got upset with me for spending too much time with my cousins gambling, so she locked me out of the house one evening. I'm in an apartment for a while. I'll move back home in a couple of years. I'm staying away long enough to let Shirley see that she needs me at home."

"David and I never fight," Maria said. "But I can tell that at times we feel bored since our son, Jonathan, is no longer here at home."

"I never knew you liked white men," Lenny said.

"David's not white. He's Jewish."

"He looks white to me."

"He's Jewish. There is a difference."

"Gladys Knight's brother, Merald, really liked you when you were at Motown. I thought you would have married him."

"He was a very nice person, but I had a crush on Greg Richmond."

"And Greg got married a couple of years after he began working for Motown."

"Yes, I know."

"And you know those singers and musicians have a lot of women around them all the time," Lenny said in a warning tone. "And those women are willing to do anything for them."

"Yes, I know," Maria reluctantly acknowledged.

"So, you probably did the right thing by marrying this Jewish man ... I guess. I mean, you seem content."

"I am." Maria smiled warmly.

"Well, I've got to get to work," Lenny said and stood up. "Thanks for breakfast, and I'm glad we had a chance to talk."

"Me too."

Maria walked Lenny to the door, and before opening the door, he kissed her passionately. She was shocked and surprised by his emotions.

When they broke free, he said, "Merald Knight wasn't the only one who admired you."

Maria stared at Lenny in shock as he opened the door and walked outside, closing the door behind him. Maria stood motionlessly at the door, thinking deeply. She didn't want to fire Lenny; he had made her an offer she couldn't refuse by volunteering to take care of her yard work for free, but if he ever touched her again, she would have very strong words for him.

CHAPTER 14

A year passed, and the next summer went by very peacefully. Maria was on edge all summer, wondering if Lenny would try to kiss her again, but he never did, and David always commented on the excellent way he cared for their lawn, so she wasn't about to mention the kiss to him; she wouldn't dare act that stupidly. David would have definitely fired Lenny, and then he'd worry about any lawn man who worked for them. She concealed the kiss from him and dealt with Lenny in a strictly businesslike manner.

During the fall, Maria and David flew to Hawaii to attend Jonathan and Nicole's wedding.

The wedding was absolutely beautiful. Maria thought Nicole looked like an angel. She was very happy for Jonathan. She took more than twenty photos of them and Nicole's parents and the wedding party. The reception was on the grounds of the chapel, where there were long tables filled with food, and there were flower gardens and palm trees. A four-piece ensemble played Hawaiian music, and beautiful Hawaiian women danced.

Maria and David stayed at the Sunset Inn on the island. They had a very large room with a view of plush gardens where doves and chickadees flocked. Maria felt she was in heaven in Honolulu. The sky was a brilliant blue, and the air was fresh and sweet. David wore colorful Hawaiian shirts and sandals every day. Maria had to laugh at how her professor-husband had transformed his appearance to blend with the islanders.

In the evenings they went swimming at a gorgeous beach, and during the day they went to several festive luncheons. They also boarded small cruise ships and toured neighboring islands. It was fascinating to them to travel through vast waters and land on a remarkable small island with friendly people, waterfalls, plush greenery, and good food.

At the end of each day, they would relax on the balcony that extended from their room at the inn and take in the beauty of flowers, plants, birds, and ponds. Maria knew that she and David would have to visit the island at least once every three years.

Over the next six years, David and Maria's lives increased abundantly. Jonathan and Nicole had three children, two boys and a girl, and the couple had made three trips to Hawaii. They were very proud of their grandchildren—their grandsons Shelton and Aiden, and their granddaughter, Julie. The children were born two years apart. Nicole's mother cared for them while Jonathan and Nicole were at work.

CHAPTER 15

Lenny remained a very faithful lawn-care man. Maria never had any problems with him, and David often gave him a bonus at the end of every summer. He had been separated from his wife, Shirley, for two years, but had returned home because Shirley wanted him there to help care for their grandchildren. Their son had two children, and their daughter had four.

Lenny made himself useful in helping his grandchildren to get to school every morning, but after a few years, he ended up in the doghouse once again, and he told Maria that he and Shirley had separated again.

"So, now where do you live?" Maria asked him. He was a very faithful lawn-care man, and she didn't want to lose him.

"In the attic," Lenny said.

"In the attic where, Lenny?" Maria sharply asked him.

"At my house," he replied, with a sound of irritation in his voice. He leaned against the handle of his lawnmower and took in a deep breath. "It's furnished," he added, deciding that his situation wasn't quite that bad. "I have a nice bed."

Maria laughed. "And you call that a separation?"

"We are separated, but I still do my part. I take the grandchildren to school, and I pay all of the bills at home, but I be damn if I give up going to my cousin's house on the weekends; that's asking too much of me, but Shirley doesn't give a damn. She thinks I'm supposed to do whatever she asks; that ain't about to happen."

"You probably stay out too late when you go to your cousin's," Maria said. "And you probably do a lot of drinking. I've heard about those gambling parties."

"Yeah, but so what? Shirley drinks wine, smokes, and listens to the blues. I never bother her."

"Does your brother, Andrew, go with you to your cousin's?" Maria inquired.

"No, his wife won't let him. They run the nursery, work hard together, and go home together. They both own Lincolns. They're doing good. I had to haul Shirley's ass around. She never passed driver training. She was like, 'Oh, this car is moving!' and screaming, and she just never made it through driver training, but now she has a part-time job at a mall, and one of the ladies who works with her picks her up."

"Well, good for her. But you see how Andrew avoids drinking and gambling? That's why he's doing so well, Lenny."

"That tight-ass penny-pincher is so stingy, it's pitiful!" Lenny exclaimed, standing erect. "He won't loan anyone a dime. He's lost a lot of friends. I've always had far more friends than Andrew. I don't mind helping someone when they're down on their luck. And he better not ever criticize me for gambling, whereas I own that nursery. I saved money for over thirty years in order to open a business."

"That was a great achievement, Lenny."

"Thank you, and I'm not going to accept any bullshit from Shirley or Andrew."

"I understand," Maria replied. "I have to go inside. David was shaving before I came out here to say hello to you. He's going to take me to Canada for a breakfast buffet."

"You have a fancy life being married to a professor," Lenny commented.

Maria thought deeply for a moment. She could detect the resentful tone in Lenny's voice and felt he didn't have any reasons to feel scornful. She and David treated him well, and she appreciated him as her friend.

"There's nothing fancy about the way David and I live," Maria replied.

Lenny stared at Maria for a long while as he remained silent. *Maria crossed over,* he thought. *It seems as if she has given up on her people, but she is a good person, and I have always been fond of her.* He just didn't understand why she had chosen to marry a Jewish man.

He quietly departed, slowly pushing his lawnmower toward his truck, and Maria went back inside the house.

CHAPTER 16

The following spring, Lenny did not show up at the Silvermans' home, and the grass was growing tall. David had been in Washington, DC, at the Smithsonian Institution, where he had taken his students for a week. They had a great time visiting several museums. When David returned home from the airport, he slowly drove his Buick into the driveway, observing the poorly kept lawns at home. He parked, grabbed his luggage from the trunk, and dashed inside the house. "Maria!" he called out.

"I'm in the den!"

He quickly walked into the den. Maria was stretched out on the sofa, talking on the phone, while jazz music softly played on the radio.

"Cynthia, David's home," she said to her best friend. "Okay, bye."

She hung up the phone as David set down his suitcase, and she jumped into his arms. She loved her tall, handsome husband, who had gained a few pounds over the years. He was now solid and strong, weighing 170 pounds. He frequently exercised at a gym on Saturdays.

They kissed long and hard.

"Missed me?" he asked.

"Too much," she replied.

"I'll make up for it, starting tonight." He swooned, but suddenly it concerned him as to why their lawn looked such a mess. "Why is our lawn in such bad shape?" he asked.

"I have no idea," Maria admitted. "I haven't heard from Lenny. He never answers his cell phone when I call him, and he hasn't returned any of my messages."

"You should go to his nursery and inquire about him."

"I will."

"Any dinner?"

"Yes. I broiled boneless steaks and made mashed potatoes and broccoli."

"Just what I need."

They kissed again, knowing that tonight would be blazing hot under the sheets; it was always that way whenever David had been away for a few days.

Later that evening, after they had made love and showered, the doorbell rang.

"I'll answer the door," David said as Maria sat at the dresser, drying her wet hair. "I can't imagine who would be calling on us at nine thirty in the evening," he mumbled as he slid into his robe and house shoes and headed for the front door.

"Turn on the porch light!" Maria yelled.

David swiftly walked to the door and flipped on the porch light. He noticed Lenny standing at the door, looking really down on his luck. He opened the door. "Lenny, are you okay?" he asked.

"No, not at all. I lost my wife."

"I'm sorry. Come in."

David held the door open, and Lenny slowly walked in.

"Let's go into the living room," David said. They walked into the room, and David turned on a lamp. "Have a seat. Maria and I were worried about you."

Lenny sat on the light-blue french sofa as his eyes focused on the cream-colored carpet. The room was filled with a matching light-blue love seat and two wide swaybacked chairs in the same color.

"Maria!" David shouted. "Lenny is here."

In a few moments, Maria walked into the living room, wearing a sea-green terry-cloth dress and house slippers. Her long, damp hair hung below her shoulders. "Lenny, what's wrong?" she asked.

"Shirley died," he said, looking slightly up toward Maria. "Her funeral was on Friday."

Maria felt speechless. She merely gasped.

"We're sorry," David quickly said. "Can I get you anything? A cup of coffee or a glass of wine?"

"No, thanks. I just wanted you to know that I'm sorry I wasn't able to cut your grass."

"Oh, the hell with the yard!" David instantly replied. "What happened to your wife?"

"She had cirrhosis," Lenny said, looking David straight in his eyes. "I can't lie. She was at home all the time, drinking."

David and Maria eased onto the love seat. "She was just bored," Maria said.

"She felt it was her duty to be at home every day so that she could look after our grandchildren. Our grandchildren meant the world to her. She felt if she wasn't there to make sure they went to school on time and arrived home safely, they could get shot or kidnapped."

"That … that's understandable how she felt," David stammered. "It's hard to imagine a child being shot or kidnapped, but it does happen."

"The streets aren't safe," Maria added, "so, Shirley was doing the right thing, except she probably became depressed, being at home all the time. David and I buried his aunt and uncle a couple of years ago. They had become prisoners in their home, and then old age simply took them away."

"Well, we never know what we might have to undergo in life," Lenny said. "I can come by on Wednesday or Thursday to cut your grass."

"Whenever you care to, Lenny," David said.

"We're so sorry for your loss," Maria tearfully added. "Shirley really loved her grandchildren. I remember how you always drove them to school. She made sure they were safe."

"Yes, she did," Lenny sadly replied. "I'll be here on Thursday and cut your grass."

"Okay, that's fine," David said. "And, I'm always here if you need to talk."

"Thank you. I must be going."

"Take care, Lenny," Maria said as he walked to the door and let himself out.

"I feel so sorry for him," Maria sobbed.

"Come on, darling," David said, standing and taking Maria by the hand. "I know Lenny has a big heart, but he also has a lot of willpower. He'll be okay."

They walked back to their bedroom, dressed for bed, and once in bed, they snuggled close together.

CHAPTER 17

Lenny cut the Silvermans' grass that Thursday morning. He was full of vigor and happy that spring had arrived in late April. In Detroit, spring was often so short, it was almost nonexistent. Lenny always rejoiced in the brevity of the spring season in which he could cultivate the land and plant many flowers and plants and create gardens for luxury homes. All of his creative energy surged forth in April and stayed with him until late fall. He thought about Shirley with every breath he took and during every moment he planted new bulbs. He knew she would live within his heart throughout his life.

He always worked extra hard before the summer thunderstorms erupted and made it too dangerous to be outdoors. But as soon as the grounds dried, he was back to work, being creative in making yards and gardens look their finest. He loved working at different houses in different neighborhoods much better than merely selling products at his nursery. But in the winter, he enjoyed working in his nursery by caring for poinsettias and a variety of plants and Christmas trees.

One Saturday morning in early summer, he was busy cutting the grass in the Silvermans' backyard when he noticed David walking to the garage and soon backing out in his bronze Cadillac. He no longer cared to own Buicks. Once he drove away, Lenny knew it was the perfect time to have a chat with Maria. He rang the doorbell at the side door, and Maria answered the door. She was wearing denim capris and a white short-sleeved top. Her beautiful black hair flowed over her shoulders. Lenny loved admiring how good she always looked.

"Hi, Lenny," she said, warmly smiling, thankful that Lenny did not let anything spoil his joy in life and that he was able to roll with the punches after losing Shirley.

"Can I come in?"

"Sure."

Lenny stepped inside. "We haven't talked in a while."

"No, we haven't, but I have a dentist appointment at eleven."

"So, we can talk for a few minutes. It's only nine fifteen," Lenny said.

"Okay, let's go into the kitchen."

Lenny sat at the kitchen table. Maria poured him a cup of coffee and gave it to him. He added cream and sugar, which were on the table. Maria set a blueberry scone in front of him.

"Thanks for the pastry," he said. "I skipped breakfast and started working at seven this morning."

"You should never skip breakfast," Maria lectured him.

"I know, but I was anxious to get out of the house."

"Because you miss Shirley?"

"Yes, I really do. So, where did David go?"

"To the barber," Maria said, pouring herself a cup of coffee. "And then he's heading to Southfield to shop at the big and tall men's store." She sat at the table.

"You probably know that Greg Richmond and the Soul Invaders will be at Chene Park in two weeks," Lenny said.

"Oh my God, no, I didn't know! I haven't turned on the radio in a few days. I love Chene Park, and it would be wonderful to see Greg."

"I knew you would be happy to know he's coming here. He and his band will open up the show for Freddie Jackson."

"Oh my goodness, Freddie Jackson! I have to call my best friend, Cynthia, and ask her to go to the concert with me. We work together, and she's always been a fan of Freddie Jackson."

Lenny slowly ate his scone. "I know you said your husband loves classical music."

CHAPTER 18

Maria thought deeply for a moment as she sipped her coffee. *My, how the years had flown!* At one time in her life, she was actually there on Motown's premises, rubbing shoulders with all those famous singers, songwriters, producers, and musicians, and then she was in the heart of the Cultural Center, working at Wayne State and taking evening classes. She could never in a million years regret how she met David and fell in love with him. It never mattered to her that he was Jewish; so many black men had married white women, and there hadn't been a single black man who had warmed up to her and expressed an interest in her becoming his wife. David was far too special to her to allow race to become an issue in their lives; it had never been an issue between them, and she knew it should never become an issue. They were happily married.

She slowly sipped her coffee and eyed Lenny. He was playing the devil's advocate, very subtly but also very effectively.

"David also enjoys Motown's music," she finally answered him. "He likes Smokey and Diana."

"But he wouldn't sit through a Freddie Jackson concert," Lenny said as he finished his scone.

"No, he wouldn't."

"My friend, Charles Haley, who plays guitar in Greg's band, told me they are staying at the Westin Hotel near Chene Park on the river. Downtown is going to be really crowded on the night of that concert.

Charles said they are going to spend three weeks at the Westin so everyone in the band can visit their families."

"Are you going to the concert?"

"No. I'm keeping my grandchildren for my son and my daughter. They're going to the car races in Indianapolis."

Maria refilled their cups with coffee.

"That sounds really exciting," she said, thinking how she had never been to the races. "So, are your grandchildren doing okay?"

"They're doing good. They worried me to death about why Shirley passed away, but they've finally gotten over it. My son and daughter work hard to provide for them, so I never mind taking care of them when they want to take a special trip."

"I'm glad they're doing well, and thank you for telling me about the concert. Greg hasn't performed here in Detroit in many years."

Lenny's eyes twinkled. "And yet you still have a crush on him."

Maria blushed; the truth seemed to hit her straight in her stomach. "He reminds me of the good old days at Motown. Everything was so exciting back then. You know as well as I do, Lenny, how much fun we had."

They slowly sipped their coffee.

"Of course, I remember," Lenny replied, full of spunk, "but those days have ended. We no longer work for Motown. We're in a new millennium. Thank God we were able to survive that attack on the World Trade Center."

"That was horrifying," Maria responded. "It was as if terrorists were trying to destroy the free world. But Diana Ross, Smokey, Stevie, the Temptations, and other artists who worked for Motown are still performing."

"And you still have a crush on Greg Richmond."

"A mild one. So what? You had a crush on Tammi Terrell."

"Yeah, that's true," Lenny sheepishly admitted, "but I couldn't compete with her singing partner, Marvin Gaye. He was really crazy about her, but it broke his heart when she got involved with David Ruffin."

"David was a dynamic leader of the Temptations, but his temper was out of control," Maria stated.

"He may have caused Tammi's death," Lenny said and quickly finished his coffee. "Well, I've gotta go. If you go to that concert, let me know about it."

"I sure will."

Lenny swiftly walked to the door and let himself out.

CHAPTER 19

A couple of weeks later, Maria and her best friend, Cynthia Alridge, who was a financial manager at the Graduate School of Social Work, were seated among a crowd on the river in Chene Park, the beautiful outdoor concert theater in Detroit. Cynthia was a Freddie Jackson die hard.

"I can't believe I'm at one of Freddie's concerts!" Cynthia squealed as they sat in the center of the theater.

"I can't believe I'll get to see Greg perform," Maria confessed and then added, "I know this will sound strange, but Greg reminds me of Yul Brynner."

"What?" Cynthia laughed. "That Egyptian man who was the star of *The King and I*?"

"Yes, that was Yul. I've never known his nationality, but Lord, that man had a powerful physique, a real sexy swagger, and a confident look that could melt a glacier."

"And you feel Greg is like him?"

"Most definitely, by the way he stands, all that confidence he exudes, and he has so much finesse that he just blows me away!"

Cynthia laughed. "Have you ever told David how much you admire Greg Richmond?"

"No, never. Do you think I'm crazy?"

Cynthia laughed harder. "Well, Richard knows I love Freddie Jackson, and he doesn't care. He's into jazz, and he doesn't care anything about Freddie."

"When David and I first married, he had several magazines with articles on Sophia Loren. He told me he deeply admired her. All of us feel connected to a certain celebrity. They inspire us."

"Yes, they do, but you conceal your crush on Greg from David."

"It's no big deal; it's just a mild crush," Maria whispered as she noticed the concert announcer walking across the stage.

"Ladies and gentlemen," the announcer said in a loud, clear voice into the mike, "welcome to the Freddie Jackson concert, also featuring Greg Richmond and the Soul Invaders!"

Everyone clapped and cheered.

"Greg Richmond and his band will start the show in exactly five minutes. After the band's performance, there will be a twenty-minute break, and following the break, Mr. Freddie Jackson will come on and perform for an hour and twenty minutes."

"All right!" a lady screamed.

"Bring it on!" another lady yelled.

"This concert is brought to you by the Ford Motor Company, the Chrysler Corporation, and Coca-Cola. These sponsors have made it possible for Detroit to prosper both culturally and economically over many decades. Most of you know that Mr. Greg Richmond began his musical career right here in Detroit at Motown Records in the early 1960s. He now lives in California. He is one of the world's preeminent trumpeters. Let's give it up for Greg Richmond and the Soul Invaders!"

Everyone shouted and clapped as a thunderous noise roared throughout the open theater on the river. It was a glorious day, and several boaters drifted close to the arena and idled so that they could view the concert.

Moments later, Greg Richmond walked onto the stage, carrying his bright, shining trumpet, and his band members followed behind him—Pete Norris on the drums, Al Brenton on keyboard, Charles Haley on guitar, and Mike Carter on the saxophone.

"Ladies and gentlemen, good evening," Greg said into the microphone. "It's certainly good to be here in Detroit, my hometown."

"Oh my God, Greg's voice is so rich and warm!" Maria exclaimed.

"It certainly is," Cynthia agreed.

There was thunderous applause.

"Anytime the media covers a city a hundred times in one month, you know it's a great city," Greg continued.

"Right on, bro!" a deep male voice shouted.

"Detroit has paved the way for the world to make progress in automotive manufacturing, industry, science, medicine, environmental studies and advancements, and in the world of music, it has produced many megastars, and I have been very fortunate that I was born here in Detroit and received my start in music at the Motown Record Corporation."

The audience shouted praises and clapped endlessly.

As soon as the audience quieted, Greg said, "And now, I'd like to play for you 'Brazilian Nights,' which is on our newly released CD."

Maria felt herself swept away by Greg's beautiful music and his powerful, sexy stance as he blasted away on his trumpet. After "Brazilian Nights," he and his band continued to play their most popular tunes, which included "Midnight Fever," "Harlem Heat," "Love Is the Answer," and "The El Train." Midway through the band's performance, Greg introduced all of his band members.

After Greg Richmond and the Soul Invaders finished their performance, an intermission followed, and soon, Freddie Jackson appeared on stage, looking radiant in a navy suit, with a white shirt opened to expose his chest, and a gold chain. He began pouring out his warm, romantic love songs, which flowed throughout the night in the crowded arena and across the darkened waters. Freddie's songs soothed hearts, and women swooned over the gentle, tender songs of love. Freddie's singing filled them with hope and joy and refreshed their spirits.

CHAPTER 20

After the concert, Maria returned home and found David asleep in bed. She was happy he didn't mind her going out with Cynthia. He was a kind and generous man and didn't mind allowing her to embrace her culture. She tolerated his classical music, and he never interfered in her love for R&B music.

For several days after the concert, Maria thought about those glorious days that she'd spent on Motown's campus. She could hear Jimmy Ruffin singing, "What Becomes of the Brokenhearted," the Elgins pouring out "Darling Baby," the Temptations soulfully singing "My Girl," Marvin Gaye and Tammi Terrell belting out "Your Precious Love," the Four Tops' crisp voices rendering "I Can't Help Myself," and the Supremes declaring in song, "Stop! In the Name of Love." Those songs and so many others flooded Maria's mind. She remembered the picnics and Christmas parties that Berry Gordy provided for his employees, and boy, could Berry throw a party; he spared no expense.

She could also envision Stevie Wonder playing his harmonica, Junior Walker blowing his saxophone, and all the dynamic gusto wrapped up in Junior Walker, and she would forever envision Greg Richmond pumping away on his trumpet.

She treasured the memories she had of Motown, but she knew that Berry Gordy had set his sights on California, and she had to establish a life for herself in Michigan. David was her key to life, and yet she felt she had to connect with Greg in order to embrace an essential part of her life, the great love she had for that golden past on Motown's campus.

She knew her husband connected quite well with his Jewish heritage on Wayne State's campus. Jewish professors were quite prominent there. Out of fifty-eight professors in the Graduate School of Social Work, fifty were Jews, and many other Jewish professors worked at the university; Maria realized her husband was in a rich environment. She could not see any reason why she should not reach out and make contact with Greg.

After a few days of deliberating about contacting Greg, Maria courageously called the Westin Hotel in downtown Detroit and asked to be connected to Greg Richmond's room. In a few moments, Greg answered the phone.

"This is Greg," he answered.

Maria felt her heart racing away. "Greg, it's Maria Silverman."

There was silence for a few moments, then he asked, "Have we met?"

"Yes, of course, Greg. You knew me when I worked at Motown. I often saw you at the Hitsville office. My last name was Arlington."

"Oh my God, Maria! What a surprise! I saw you a few years ago at the airport in LA. You were with your son."

"Yes, and it was good seeing you also. I saw your performance in Chene Park. Your band is fabulous. I loved everything you played."

"Why, thank you. I'm glad you enjoy our music. So, when did your name change to Silverman?"

"When I married David Silverman a few years after I left Motown. He's a history professor at Wayne State."

"And do you teach?"

"No, I'm a supervisor in the admissions office at the Graduate School of Social Work at Wayne."

"So, you met your husband while you were working there?"

"Yes, I did. And how's your wife, Carolyn? I heard that you had married her in the fall of 1967 and that you both had attended Northwestern High."

"Carolyn's doing fine. She owns a hair salon in LA, but we're no longer married. She divorced me two years ago. She never liked how much I have to travel, and that's really the life of a musician."

"I understand," Maria replied. "Lenny told me you were staying at the Westin, and so I wanted to call you and say hello."

"Lenny Jackson?" Greg asked, almost in disbelief.

"Yes."

"Lenny who drove the Gordys wherever they needed to go, and was also Stevie's personal chauffeur?"

"Yes, we both know Lenny, Greg." Maria laughed. "He moved back here to Detroit in the early nineties, and he owns a large nursery on Eight Mile Road, where he sells plants and flowers."

"Good old Lenny," Greg responded warmly. "He was always willing to help the artists in any way he could. Tell him hello for me."

"I will."

"I'd like to have lunch with you, Maria. I'll be here in Detroit for three weeks, and then I'll return to my home in LA. In mid-July, my band will perform in a concert in San Francisco."

"I'd enjoy having lunch with you. My husband doesn't mind me keeping in touch with old friends."

"Okay, so let's meet for lunch next Wednesday at one o'clock in the diner on the first floor here at the Westin."

"That's fine. I'll let the director of admissions at my job know that I have a special engagement to make next Wednesday, and she won't mind me taking an extra hour or so for lunch. I rarely ever make any requests for time off."

"Good, so I'll see you next Wednesday at one."

CHAPTER 21

The following week, Maria drove her Mazda to the entrance of the Westin Hotel, and a valet gave her a parking ticket and parked her car for her.

She walked through the lobby and found the diner. Greg was standing near the entrance, looking exceptionally handsome in a light-gray summer suit, a white shirt, and white loafers. His light-brown skin was radiant, and his large brown eyes were sparkling like diamonds. Maria had always loved his large, captivating eyes and his warm smile. His thick, coarse, dark-brown hair was neatly cut, and his mustache was perfectly trimmed. After quickly glancing Greg over, Maria knew in her heart that she had always admired him for his class, intelligence, and good looks, which was the image she had held of him in her memory for many years.

"Maria, it's good to see you," Greg said, noticing how lovely she looked in a light-gold silk dress with a long string of pearls draped around her neck. He thought she was still a superfine lady, with long, silky black hair; a delicate face; and the gentlest eyes he had ever seen.

Maria smiled warmly. "It's good to see you also, Greg," she said.

"Let's go inside."

Greg opened the door to the diner, and they walked in. A hostess quickly seated them and handed them their menus. In a few minutes, they both decided on baked salmon and potatoes au gratin. They also ordered white wine.

"It seems like a century since we've been in each other's company," Greg commented as they slowly dined.

"Yes, I know," Maria replied, fascinated by the fact that after so many years, she was finally able to spend time with Greg. She had always admired him as a brilliant musician but had never had an opportunity to converse with him. They had merely seen each other in passing when they worked together decades ago.

"I remember how we used to see each other at lunchtime when we worked at Motown, at that corner café that was always super crowded," Maria remarked.

"Dunn's Café," Greg said. "Everyone packed in there at noon; it was crazy. There was barely room to breathe."

"I know!" Maria laughed. "I remember one day Pops Gordy was standing at the counter, in back of a crowd of people, and he said you have to pray that someone waits on you."

"Pops was right." Greg chuckled. "He was head of the Gordy family, and he was often in Dunn's getting food for Berry."

"It's amazing how much time has passed," Maria continued. "It was in the late sixties when I used to walk to Dunn's for lunch, and now, here we are in 2005."

Greg paused for a moment, stared at Maria, and gently smiled. "And you're still as beautiful as ever," he said.

"Thank you, Greg."

"I plan to return to Detroit in about five years and live here permanently," he informed Maria. "I plan to work in a recording studio. I don't care to travel forever. You should come to LA and let me show you around."

"I was there a few years ago. How is your son?"

"He graduated from UCLA. He's now married and living in Hawaii."

"Good for him. My sons are twins, and they live close to me. You should come to LA and let me show you the fine nightclubs and supper clubs that we have and the beautiful beaches."

"I'd love to see all that, but I am married, Greg, and if I came to LA, I'd stay at a hotel."

"Of course, that's not a problem! I'd be able to show you where Berry lives in Malibu, and I can drive you by Diana Ross's home in Beverly Hills. Stevie and Smokey are also in LA, and they don't live that far from me. You'd enjoy yourself," Greg assured her.

"I'd love to visit LA and see everyone's homes," Maria responded, thinking how wonderful it would be to see the heights of everyone's success and the enormous blessings they had received.

The waiter walked up and removed their empty plates and set down their check. They slowly sipped their wine, and Maria felt thrilled over being up close and personal with Greg. He was flattered to know that after so many years, she felt some attraction to him. He assumed that her life with the professor must have been rather boring.

Soon, the waiter returned, and Greg paid him in cash and told him to keep the change. The man smiled graciously and happily departed.

"Let me give you my cell phone number," Greg said.

"Sure." Maria quickly took a pen and a sheet of paper from her purse and wrote down Greg's name and number.

"Call me at any time," he said as she put the paper and pen into her purse. "I have voice mail. And think about visiting me in October. I'll be in San Francisco next month. In August, I'll be in Vegas, and in September, I'll be in Dallas."

"I shouldn't have a problem visiting you in October. I'll tell my husband, David, that I'm going to LA to visit old friends from Motown. He wouldn't mind. He travels a lot with his students at Wayne State, and he wouldn't mind allowing me to travel to meet with old friends."

CHAPTER 22

Greg was pleased to know that Maria was just as anxious to be with him as he was to be with her, but he also keenly detected her dedication to her husband. He felt in time he could break down that barrier between the two of them. He had been able to lure a few women away from their husbands, especially those who were in unpleasant situations, but with Maria, it seemed that she was primarily very bored. Boredom was good, he thought. He knew how to bring on the magic, how to relax and let his charisma work for him.

He smiled to himself for a moment and said, "I look forward to seeing you in October. Call me and let me know a month in advance when you will arrive and where you'll be staying. I'll pick you up, and I assure you you'll enjoy your stay."

Maria wondered for a moment if Greg thought she would be so excited about spending time with him in LA that she'd forget her bond with her husband or more importantly her loyalty to him. Never, she told herself. David was a good man, and even though she felt the need for fulfillment by experiencing a side of life she had not been able to enjoy—that was, knowing what it was like to be with a celebrity—she would not sacrifice her marriage for a few days of fun in LA.

They finished their drinks and left the diner. While strolling through the lobby, Maria said, "I work very hard in September, planning orientation for over three hundred students, but things are much more settled in October, and I can request a vacation during the second week in October. I'll call you during the last week in September and confirm my travel date and arrival time in LA."

"That will be excellent. I enjoy my home in LA. I'm on the outskirts of the city on a hill overlooking a valley, and I have a swimming pool."

"That sounds beautiful," Maria said.

"My sons, Antonio and Mario, live near me. Mario lives in an apartment, but he is at my home a lot so he can swim in my pool and hang out, so as to avoid his girlfriend who is pressuring him to marry her. Antonio is much more settled than Mario. He's married and has three children. He's a bank manager. Mario is a computer analyst and is always on the go, helping people to resolve their computer problems."

"You must have been really delighted to have twins," Maria said as they neared the entrance.

"That was a huge surprise, but, yes, I was very happy. Antonio is a bit taller than me, and he's my complexion. Mario is my height, five-ten, but he's fair-skinned like his mother."

"My son, Jonathan, is very tall like his father. He and his wife live in Hawaii. She's Hawaiian, and they have three children. David and I have been to visit them several times."

"I know you loved being in Hawaii. Where does Jonathan work?"

"He and his wife are both environmentalists, and they work for the Department of Natural Resources in Honolulu."

"That's very good," Greg commented. They stepped out front, and Greg signaled for the valet, who rushed up to them. Maria gave him her parking ticket, and he darted off. A few minutes later, Maria's Mazda appeared before her. Greg bid her farewell as she got in and drove off.

A week later, Maria told David she had talked with a few of her friends in Los Angeles whom she had known when they worked at Motown, and they thought it would be a good idea for them to meet in October and enjoy a small reunion. David told her it would be good for her to meet with her friends and that they would certainly have a lot to discuss. Maria said she would spend ten days in LA and that she would request a vacation from work. She did have three friends who were former coworkers at Motown who lived in LA, and she would contact them and make arrangements to meet with them when she arrived in the city. She knew it was necessary to make contact with her friends at the time she planned to visit Greg so that she could prove to David that she was actually meeting with old buddies.

CHAPTER 23

October seemed to arrive a lot sooner than Maria anticipated, and she was overly nervous about flying such a long distance to meet with Greg. Her friends agreed to have lunch with her one day while she was there, and they would also spend a day shopping together.

David drove her to the airport. She had phoned Greg, and he would meet her at the airport once she arrived. When David kissed her goodbye, her body was shaking, and he stared her intently in her eyes. "Dear, are you afraid of flying alone?" he asked.

"No, sweetheart. I'm just excited and anxious. I can't believe I'll be reuniting with old friends after all these years," she responded.

David laughed. "You'll be just fine. And I'm glad you packed lightly. Some people load themselves down with luggage, and it's hard to maneuver through a crowded terminal with a lot of luggage."

"That's so true, David." She could barely stand to look him in the eyes. "Well, I'll get inside and wait for my flight."

They kissed again, very briefly, and the baggage attendant took her large suitcase and wardrobe bag before she darted inside the terminal. After a forty-minute wait to board her flight, she lined up with passengers heading to Los Angeles on Delta flight 126, departing at 10:30 a.m.

Once she was comfortably seated on the airplane, the flight attendant gave instructions about the oxygen masks and having seatbelts fastened. Soon Maria felt the plane lifting and climbing upward into the sky, and when it began cruising through clouds, she relaxed and began thinking about her loving husband. She accepted coffee and a doughnut from an attendant, and as she slowly sipped her coffee and nibbled on her doughnut, she thought about all the warm love she had shared with David over the years, and she never regretted one moment being with him. The elderly couple who sat next to her were sipping their coffee and talking privately with each other. Her mind was fully absorbed by thinking about David, so the elderly couple were almost oblivious to her.

David had been so nervous when she first met him that she could understand why he had been somewhat of a loner and had not dated in a long while. She was certain that his nervousness and shyness had caused women to simply ignore him, but she could relate to his aloneness. Black men had deserted black women. After the war in Vietnam, a lot of black men had decided that one of the best ways to succeed in America would be to partner with white women. White women were easily accessible and anxious to be with black men, and black men felt that they were their ticket to success in America. White women fueled a campaign against black women by declaring them to be unkind and unappreciative of black men, which was their way of justifying why they were with black men.

Maria slowly ate her doughnut, absorbed in thought. *America is a country divided against itself,* she thought. *The white man wishes to remain in complete control, and through his politics and greed, he has divided the nation. We are all merely people, but wars have plundered us to the point that we can barely survive. David and I are merely people. He is more than just a Jew, and I am more than just a black. We are people who were created by God, and God is a God of love, not hate.*

"The doughnuts are decent," the elderly white lady next to Maria said to her.

"Oh, they are." Maria smiled as she abandoned her deep thoughts.

"Do you have family in Los Angeles?"

"No, friends I haven't seen in a long while."

"Hmmm," the elderly woman said as her small eyes peered at Maria, and Maria felt that the woman knew she was actually going to LA to meet a man. *How on earth could she know that?* Maria privately scolded herself.

The four-and-a-half-hour flight went very smoothly, and soon Maria was at LAX airport, inside the terminal, where she met Greg at the Delta ticket counter.

CHAPTER 24

On the day of Maria's flight to Los Angeles, David received a surprise visit from his good friend Nelson Weinstein while he was relaxing in his living room, reading the newspaper. Nelson rang his bell at a quarter past seven.

"Nelson! My God, man, I haven't seen you in a long while! Come in."

"It has been a few years," Nelson said as he followed David into the living room.

"Have a seat."

Nelson sat on the love seat, since David had spread his newspaper on the sofa.

"We haven't talked since your uncle Isaac and aunt Sybil passed away, just a month apart from each other," Nelson said. He was quite tall and strongly built. David noted that he was still an immaculate dresser who was exceptionally particular about his appearance and spent far too much money on his clothing. But they were close friends, like brothers, really, and David always kept his opinions about Nelson's excessive spending to himself.

"Yes, it's been several years since we've seen each other, in fact," David commented.

"Time passes so quickly," Nelson said. "Do you mind if I smoke?"

David froze for a moment. "Are you still smoking cigars?" he inquired.

"Yes, of course," Nelson replied, "but if you'd rather I not smoke, I can wait until later."

"No, it's okay. Let me go into the kitchen and find you an ashtray."

David left the room, and a few minutes later, he returned and handed Nelson an ashtray. He quickly lit up. Once he began puffing on his cigar, David thought he'd choke. His face turned red. He sat down, and picked up a section of his newspaper, and glanced it over.

"I thought I'd stop in to see you, since I haven't seen you in a long while. You know I have four children, and they truly keep me busy, and Helen is a pain in the ass, God bless her soul," Nelson declared as he took a deep puff on his cigar, and David flinched. "She is always complaining about her back or her aching joints. She acts like she's ninety rather than fifty-seven." Nelson paused for a moment, "So, where is your lovely wife?"

"She's in Los Angeles. She left this morning. I took her to the airport."

"What a coincidence!" Nelson exclaimed. "I leave for Los Angeles in two days on a business trip. You know the accounting firm where I work often sends me to other cities to check on our clients. We handle accounting work for several large film-production companies, and so I've booked a room at a Hilton hotel in Universal City."

"That is truly a coincidence, Nelson. Maria is also staying at a Hilton in Universal City."

"Well, if I see her, I will definitely say hello to her. Does she have family in Los Angeles?"

"No, you remember I told you she once worked for Motown Records. She's gone there to meet with old friends she worked with at Motown."

"I'll certainly say hello to her if I see her."

"And don't get fresh with her."

"Honestly, David, you should know me better than that," Nelson replied.

"I know you too well," David responded. "We were roommates at Eastern, and you were quite the player, but you were also quite studious, and I recommended you to Uncle Isaac to work in his insurance company as an accountant."

"You helped me land my first job, which was boring as hell," Nelson said, knocking ashes into the ashtray. "And you're going to feel bored with Maria being away. How is Jonathan and his family?"

"They're doing good. He and his wife love their work as environmentalists, and their three children are doing fine."

"Is he coming to visit you?"

"Yes. He and his family will be here at Christmas, and they're going to stay with us until December 28."

CHAPTER 25

Nelson's dark eyes became pensive as deep thoughts overcame him. He and David were getting older. The gray hair at his temples was proof of that fact. And Maria was no longer a spring chicken; indeed, she was younger than David, but she could certainly feel herself growing older, and it had to have been a challenge for her and David to keep their love nest hot and exciting. Sometimes a person felt a need to venture out and find ways to bring some excitement to their lives. He wondered if Maria had escaped to Los Angeles in order to have a fling with someone and add a bit of excitement to her life.

"I know you'll be glad to see Jonathan and his family," Nelson said, holding on to his main thoughts.

"Yes, of course," David quickly replied, as he finished reading an article about the number of US troops in Iraq and how the US intended to establish a democracy there.

"Is it always this quiet here at your home?" Nelson asked.

"Once I play my classical music, I forget all about the quietness," he said.

Nelson was silent for a moment as he squashed out his cigar. "David, do you suppose Maria went to LA in order to meet some man she once knew at Motown?" Nelson's thick lips trembled. He had often admired his best friend's easygoing lifestyle, even his shyness, but he wondered if he was a bit too naive in regard to his wife.

David looked startled. "Now you're beginning to remind me of my mother, Nelson."

"I don't mean to seem like a nosey old woman who doesn't trust anyone, but you know, you and Maria do face an empty nest," Nelson bluntly admitted.

"Yes, well, we're not about to have any more children, and even if there is some man that Maria might admire, which I seriously doubt, but if there is, well, he lives in LA, and we live here in Detroit."

"But you know people in the entertainment world travel a lot. They're used to covering long distances."

"Maybe they are, but Maria isn't. Besides, if she had known some man at Motown, she would have remained with that company, but she left there and became completely dedicated to her life at the university."

Nelson smiled. "Man, I'm glad you have such a good marriage. If Helen didn't complain so much, I'd feel just as good as you do, but personally, I'm always glad to get away from her nagging voice." Nelson stood up. "I've got to go now, and if I see Maria when I'm in LA, I'll say hello to her."

David shook Nelson's hand. "Okay, that's fine. Have a nice trip, and stay in touch."

"Thanks, old buddy."

David walked Nelson to the door, and he departed.

CHAPTER 26

On Nelson's third day in Los Angeles, he decided to drive around in Hollywood late one evening to view the sights. It was fascinating to him to see the girls working nearly every corner, dressed in all sorts of revealing outfits and painted up like Geisha girls. He wondered how those women felt from day to day, not knowing who they might meet or what kind of weird things they might have to do in order to make a living. The pimps were the ones who seemed to have the much easier jobs. And there were the gays and the addicts who were obviously having it just as rough as the girls.

Nelson noticed Maria Silverman exiting the Brown Derby restaurant in a less-crowded area of Hollywood, and a handsome man exited alongside her. He couldn't believe his eyes. She and the man were well dressed. It seemed as if he might have been some type of executive. Maybe Maria was curious about living in Los Angeles and knowing about what type of office work was available. Nelson drove slowly and noticed Maria and the man walking into the parking lot next to the restaurant. He pulled his rental car to the side of the street, into an available parking spot, and waited until they exited the parking lot. In a few moments, he noticed them in a silver Bentley, with the man behind the steering wheel. *Well, if he is an executive,* Nelson thought, *I'd sure like to find out what company he's working for. That's a damn expensive Bentley he's driving.*

Nelson pulled out behind them and followed them for several blocks until they came to the Hilton Hotel. He continued to follow them to the very hotel where he was staying, and he waited in back of them for the valet. As soon as the man got out of his car and accepted a parking ticket from the valet, Nelson quickly exited his car. Maria got out of the car, and she and the man proceeded inside the Hilton. Nelson approached the valet and asked for a parking ticket, received one, and rushed inside the Hilton, just in time to see Maria and the man walking toward the elevators. He slowly followed behind them, and he noticed them getting on an elevator. He got on with them, careful to stand in a corner in back of them. The man pressed for the twelfth floor, and the elevator sailed up and stopped on the fourth floor. Three teenage boys got on, talking loudly about how much fun they had at the pool. One of the boys pressed for the fourteenth floor, and Nelson was grateful they would remain on the elevator until he exited on the twelfth floor, in back of Maria and the man. When he got off, he followed several feet in back of them and stood at the end of the hallway to notice if the man was going inside the room with Maria. He did not. He talked with her for a few minutes and then departed her door. Nelson immediately pressed for an elevator, but by the time it arrived, the man stood near him.

"You're going back down to the first floor?" the man inquired. He had noticed the gentleman when they exited the elevator.

"Yes, I left a package in my car."

"I see."

"I'm new to the city," Nelson went on, "but it seems as if I've seen you before."

"That's very possible," the man replied. "I'm Greg Richmond. I have a band called Greg Richmond and the Soul Invaders."

"Oh, yes, yes, yes. I know who you are. I've seen you on that cable channel called Jazz around Town."

"So, you live in Chicago?"

"Yes, that's right. I'm Harry Goldman," Nelson lied. "I'm here for a few days visiting family."

An elevator arrived, and they got on.

"So, how do you like LA?" Greg asked.

"It's pretty fascinating. Certainly quite widespread. How do you like it?"

"I've been living here since 1972. I used to work for Motown as a musician, and I moved here to continue working for them, but in the eighties I formed my own band. Right now, I have a few weeks that I can relax before hitting the road again, so I'm able to take an old friend around LA and show her the sights."

"Perhaps an old classmate?"

"No, she used to work at Motown. She's more or less like a groupie."

Nelson laughed, and the elevator stopped on the first floor.

"I need a drink of water," Nelson said. "It was nice meeting you. I'm sure those groupies keep you busy." He chuckled.

"Yeah, they really do," Greg said, almost as if he regretted it. "But that's the price you pay for being a celebrity."

Nelson quickly headed to the water fountain, and after he gulped down some water, he went to the elevators, and got on one that took him to his room on the seventh floor.

CHAPTER 27

Inside his room, Nelson stripped off his clothing and hung his slacks and shirt in the closet. He decided he'd sleep in his underwear, which he knew would feel more comfortable than the brand-new pajamas he had bought. He would just relax and think for a while before watching the eleven o'clock news. He felt maybe it would be a good idea to buy a throwaway camera in the morning and follow Maria for a few days, to see if she ever met with Greg Richmond again. Maybe she had decided to go out with him on this night just for old times' sake. But if he discovered that she was seeing him quite frequently, he would take pictures of them and show them to David. He felt David deserved to know what Maria was doing behind his back.

The next morning, Nelson showered and dressed. He left the hotel at eight in the morning and purchased a throwaway camera at a nearby drugstore. He then went to meet a client for an early-morning meeting regarding helping that company to structure their annual budget. The meeting ended at two o'clock, and Nelson raced back to the Hilton, eager to check on Maria. Once he was in his room, he telephoned her from his room phone; after three rings she answered.

"Hello."

"I'm sorry, I was trying to reach my aunt Gladys. She's in room 1223."

"Oh, this is room 1226," Maria responded.

"Thank you very much. I'm sorry to have bothered you."

"No problem," she said and hung up.

Nelson knew it would be impossible to know exactly when Maria might leave her hotel room, but at least he was aware that she was still in her room. Now he would have to wait to see if Greg Richmond returned to visit her again today. The only thing he could do was to buy a newspaper and sit in the lobby and wait to see if Greg returned. It was only two thirty in the afternoon, and it was possible that he might not return until as late as five or six, if they planned to dine together. He decided to wait until after three, go down to the lobby and buy a newspaper, and sit and read it for a couple of hours, if necessary.

At 3:20 p.m., Nelson put the throwaway camera in his pants pocket and left his room. He took the elevator to the lobby, where he bought a newspaper and took a seat facing the entrance. He began reading the paper, starting with articles on the first page regarding the United States' presence in Iraq, the war in Afghanistan, and President Bush's interest in the welfare of families of fallen soldiers. He had just begun reading an editorial about the astronomical expense that was crippling the United States as it attempted to police the world, when he noticed Greg Richmond entering the lobby. He held his paper up in front of him and blocked Greg from seeing his face. He knew it was unwise to follow him to the twelfth floor, so he stayed seated. He was very curious why Greg had returned to the hotel. A few minutes later, Greg and Maria entered the lobby and then exited and walked down a hallway to the Universal Gift Store.

Nelson casually strolled down to the gift store and glanced inside. He noticed Maria trying on sunglasses and allowing Greg to comment on them. He decided he should go to valet parking and get his rental car, a Chrysler 500, and be prepared to follow Greg and Maria to their destination. As soon as the valet pulled up with Nelson's car, Nelson noticed Greg and Maria entering the parking garage. He circled around the lower level of the garage, allowing Greg enough time to get his car, and then he slowly drove back to the front of the lower level, just as Greg and Maria were getting into the Bentley. They drove out of the garage, and Nelson followed behind them. Greg was driving north and soon entered the freeway, and Nelson courageously kept following them.

CHAPTER 28

After a twenty-minute drive north, Greg turned onto the Grand Valley Boulevard exit, and Nelson slowly followed behind him. Greg cruised along the boulevard for fifteen minutes, and Nelson allowed him to travel ahead of him so as not to arouse his suspicions that he was being followed. Soon, Greg made a right turn onto Meadows Drive, and Nelson slowed his car down since Meadows Drive was such a narrow street in a secluded area. Greg was at least three car lengths ahead of him when he turned onto a narrow driveway at the bottom of a hill. Nelson pulled into the driveway and proceeded to drive up the hill, even though the Bentley had vanished. Nelson felt that Greg's house must have been at the top of this hill. Once he was at the top, he spotted Greg getting out of the Bentley in the driveway of what was apparently his home, and he walked around to the passenger side and opened the car door for Maria. She exited, and they walked to the front door and entered the home. The hill was quite expansive, and Greg's home was nearly two football fields in distance away from the main road. There was a wide-open field surrounding the home. Tall shrubs were lined across the right side of the road. Nelson slowly drove down the dirt road toward the shrubs and parked his car in back of them. He noticed the side door opening at Greg's house, which was next to a gorgeous swimming pool, and a young man exited. Nelson carefully studied the face of the young man, who looked a lot like Greg. He went to the two-car garage, opened one of the doors, and soon backed out in a BMW.

The Bentley was parked in front of the other garage door. Nelson felt safely hidden from the sight of the young man as he came up the hill, kicking up dirt as he sped away.

Nelson relaxed in his car and slid a jazz CD by Rick Braun into the CD player on his dash. He let the music play softly as he patiently waited to see what Greg and Maria were up to. He thought about how he had told Greg that he had seen him on cable TV, and he had. He had watched him perform on a jazz channel in Chicago when he was visiting his sister. Boy, was he glad that he was able to converse with him, or he would have been merely a mystery man. He also enjoyed the soul-jazz music produced by Greg and his band.

Greg's 2,800-square-foot spread of a home had a modern design, constructed in white stucco, with spacious windows, french doors at the entrance, and a charcoal-gray roof. Greg told Maria, who was seated on his long, curvy burgundy sofa, that he had a surprise for her. Her eyes lit up as he left the living room, went into his bedroom, and grabbed a Saks Fifth Avenue shopping bag from his bed. He walked back into the living room and handed Maria the bag.

"Oh my God, Greg, you didn't have to buy me anything!" she gushed and quickly looked inside the bag at a red silk garment. She pulled it out of the bag and noticed it was a two-piece bikini. "Oh, no!" She laughed. "You bought me a bikini!"

"Yes, I feel you'll look great in it. I guessed your size."

Marie looked at a label inside the bottom to the bikini and it was labeled a size twelve. "You guessed my size exactly correct," she said.

"Go in the bathroom and put it on. You can leave your clothes in the bathroom. There's a hanger on a hook on the back of the bathroom door, and you can hang your clothes there. Let's go for a swim."

Maria rushed into the bathroom, which was in the hallway, and quickly stripped off her clothes and put on the bikini. She brushed her long, flowing black hair and felt she looked great in the bikini. She would take off her sandals once she was at the pool.

When she walked back into the living room, Greg was standing there in his white silk trunks, and she shivered a bit as she stared at his solid, firm body. His eyes were delighted to see how her shapely, golden-brown body looked magnificent in a red bikini, and his mind began racing, wondering if she'd spend the night with him. They walked out to the pool and dove in and began swimming.

CHAPTER 29

Nelson was standing between two shrubs, gawking at Greg and Maria as they swam like fish. He wondered how long would they swim, and after twenty minutes, he got back in his car and listened to more jazz. After a short while, he became very curious about Greg and Maria, and he quickly exited his car.

As he peered through the shrubs, he noticed them walking up a ladder, exiting the pool, and walking along the patio to a lounge chair, where they dried off with a large, white towel. Greg pulled Maria close to him, placed a hand firmly on her buttocks, and gently kissed her. Nelson snapped several photos. In an instant, Greg ran his hand inside the top to Maria's bikini and fondled her breast. Soon, her firm, round breast was exposed, and Greg kissed it. Nelson snapped away. Maria pushed Greg away from her, covered her breast, and swiftly began walking toward the house. Greg followed behind her. Nelson went back to his car to wait to see what would happen next. He was more than satisfied over the kissing scene he had caught on film, especially the way Greg had kissed Maria's breast. Nearly a half hour passed, and Nelson was startled to see Greg's Bentley just a few feet in front of him as he sped down the dirt road. Maria was seated next to him.

Nelson started his car and followed them. Soon he was back on the freeway and heading in the direction of Universal City. Nelson couldn't believe how short Maria's stay had been at Greg's home. The way he came on to her made him feel they would enjoy an evening of hot lovemaking, but he felt almost dizzy, speeding along behind them as they headed back to Universal City. After a while, they were back at the Hilton. They pulled into valet parking, and got out of the Bentley. Nelson eased into the garage, stopped in back of the Bentley, and waited only a moment until an attendant drove off in the Bentley. As he drove up to the attendants' booth, Greg and Maria were walking toward the elevator. He got out of his car, and another attendant approached him and took over his car. Greg and Maria had taken the elevator to the lobby, where they would take another elevator to Maria's floor. Nelson followed suit. When he arrived on the twelfth floor, he could hear Greg and Maria talking in the hallway, but he could not discern what they were saying. Greg was apologizing for overreacting to their leisurely swim and was assuring Maria that he would keep himself in check and that she should not allow the incident to spoil her trip.

Nelson felt Greg must have been apologizing for his brazen actions by the poolside, and that he would be intently focused on Maria as he offered his plea for forgiveness, so that would be a perfect time to snap their picture while they were standing at the door to her hotel room. Nelson wished to prove that Greg was often at Maria's room. He was developing a series of snapshots that would make it impossible for Maria to deny her involvement with Greg. He was afraid that sooner or later, Maria would give in to Greg's impulses and that he needed to warn his best friend about this Casanova who was seeking out his wife for his personal pleasure and thrills.

He quickly snapped their picture and then immediately caught an elevator to his floor. He was happy that so far, he had been successful in photographing evidence of what Maria probably considered a secret affair. But he would expose her secret so that David could chastise her and make sure she put an end to courting danger. He wasn't sure if Maria was just trying to add a bit of excitement to her life or if she was seriously attracted to this musician, but he was certain that his insatiable curiosity would eventually lead him to the right conclusion.

CHAPTER 30

The next day, Nelson left the hotel quite early in the morning, to attend a meeting at yet another film-production company. He would crunch numbers most of the day, but by the midafternoon, he would be free to check on Maria, which was becoming a fancy and satisfying sport to him, and he was especially delighted that she didn't have a clue as to what he was doing.

After spending several hours with his client, Nelson left their offices by three forty and enjoyed a late lunch at a nearby restaurant. Afterward, he returned to the Hilton and went inside Randall's Men's Leisure Wear on the first floor of the hotel and bought himself a navy cap. He decided he could disguise himself by wearing a cap and his sunglasses as he sat in the lobby or followed Greg and Maria to their destination. He left Randall's and stopped at a newspaper stand and purchased a newspaper, then sat inside the lobby and waited to observe any actions on the part of Greg or Maria.

He read the newspaper quite easily by wearing his prescription sunglasses, and he kept noticing people as they entered the lobby and walked past him. Finally, by five thirty, he spotted Maria entering the lobby. She was dressed in a lovely, straight-fitted lavender dress with a wide, white belt strapped around her waist, which accented the white cuffs on the short sleeves of the dress. Her dainty feet were clad in a comfortable pair of soft, white leather shoes that matched her large bag. Her good looks and fine appearance truly piqued his curiosity. She was walking toward the entrance, and he quickly folded his newspaper and jumped to his feet so that he could follow her.

Maria exited the hotel and began walking down the sidewalk to the north of the hotel. Nelson casually walked several feet behind her as they passed several fancy stores. After walking four long blocks, Maria came to Mozelli's Italian Restaurant and went inside. Nelson paused for a moment as he stared at the entrance to the restaurant. *Ah, so now she's meeting this character for dinner,* Nelson thought. *Pretty soon, he will be in her pants.* He waited a few moments and then entered the restaurant. A head waiter greeted him, and he explained that he simply wanted a menu to take with him; the waiter walked away to get him a menu. Nelson looked around the restaurant and noticed Maria walking to a table where three women sat, and she sat down with them. Soon, the waiter returned and gave him a menu, and he thanked him and departed the restaurant.

Outside, in the warm, glowing sun, Nelson thought, *Well, I'll be damned. Maria knows people who live here in Los Angeles. She is covering her tracks, obviously, keeping in touch with these friends so that David will feel that they were the reason why she made this journey to Los Angeles.*

Nelson walked across the street to an ice-cream parlor and ordered a banana split. He sat at a counter by a window and slowly ate the ice cream. He dreaded thinking about how long Maria might dine with old friends. *Jesus, women can talk for hours,* he privately thought. He would eat as slowly as possible and then order coffee. He imagined he could have close to a two-hour wait before Maria left that diner.

He was sweating when Maria and her friends finally exited the restaurant and stood outside, laughing and talking with each other. Maria took several pictures of them, and she had one of the ladies take pictures of her with her friends. It was nearly seven thirty when they split up and waved goodbye to Maria. Nelson was finishing his third cup of coffee, and he quickly exited the ice cream parlor, and followed Maria back to the hotel. He got on the elevator with her. She pressed for the twelfth floor, and he pressed the button for the seventh floor. When he exited the elevator and headed toward his room, he felt exasperated over the fact that he had sat for hours while she carried on with a group of women. He went into his room, stripped off his clothing, and got into the shower. He truly needed to cool off and simmer down.

CHAPTER 31

In her hotel room, Maria undressed, put on a nightshirt, and got into bed. She turned on the television and began watching a detective movie. She would call David, as she did each day, after the movie ended. She was very pleased that she had put Greg in his place when she visited him at his home. She made it firmly clear to him that she had no intentions of becoming intimate with him and that he had to respect the fact that she was married. At first, Greg felt that Maria was merely trying to seem modest by stating that she was a married woman, but he discovered that she actually took her marital vows very seriously; however, he also well knew that she had the hots for him and figured it was just a matter of time before she would give in to him.

After the movie ended, Maria turned off the TV and telephoned David. He answered, and she could hear classical music playing in the background. "Hi, honey," she said.

"Hello, love," David replied, sounding as if he wished very much that she was lying next to him. "So, how's it going?"

"Everything is lovely," she answered. "My friends and I are having a wonderful time. There's so much to see and do. Tomorrow we'll drive around San Fernando Valley and look at all the gorgeous homes there that are owned by famous people. We'll also drive around Malibu and enjoy the wonderful scenery."

"I know you have always longed to see how Motown's artists live in California and that this is a dream come true for you," David responded, "so enjoy your exciting vacation. We'll have our own special reunion when you return home."

"That will be better than being away from home," Maria admitted. "California is like a fantasy life, and I much prefer being at home with you."

"I'm glad to hear that, darling," David said. "Be sweet. I love you."

"I love you too."

They hung up, and a few minutes later, Maria fell sound asleep.

The next morning, Greg called her to remind her that he would pick her up so he could take her around LA and show her the homes of the rich and famous. He would meet her in the lobby of her hotel at noon. She told him she would be ready. After they hung up, she ordered breakfast from room service, and minutes later, as she ate, she felt guilty about deceiving her husband, causing him to feel that she merely wanted to reunite with old friends, whereas in actuality, she was trying to fulfill a great longing she had held within her, to know what it was like to share life with a celebrity. Greg was offering her a chance to spend time with him and to share in the glory of celebrity life. She only desired an opportunity to enjoy the fringes of the great success so many people she had known at Motown had acquired, but she had no desire at all to give up her life with her husband, who meant much more to her than all the glitter in the world.

After she finished her breakfast, she thought, *Well, today I'll be able to see the homes of those who went straight to the top of the entertainment world. That will be truly fascinating.*

At noon, she met Greg in the lobby of the hotel, and they left together for their excursion around exclusive areas in LA.

CHAPTER 32

Soon, Greg was driving his Bentley through San Fernando Valley, and he pointed out to Maria the home of Michael Jackson's family. She marveled at the gorgeous estate with all the beautiful land and trees surrounding it, and she snapped a few pictures of it. Then Greg drove her to the awesome home of Smokey Robinson, which was only a few minutes' drive from the Jacksons' home, and again, Maria was able to take more photos. Maria had noticed security men at the Jacksons' home and also here at Smokey's home, but they merely stared at her, realizing that she was some starstruck tourist.

Greg also knew that Stevie Wonder lived in close proximity, but he had failed to write down his address. He drove to Beverly Hills and pointed out the beautiful mansion owned by Diana Ross, and again, Maria took several photos. She was completely blown away to realize the great wealth of so many artists whom she had known when they were quite young—especially Stevie, whom she had met when he was only seventeen—and how they had risen to great heights and fame over the years. Her favorite singers at Motown had been David Ruffin of the Temptations and Marvin Gaye. Greg had informed Maria that many of Motown's former employees still lived in LA and that occasionally he met with them.

Soon, they were heading toward Malibu, where Berry Gordy Jr. lived in a magnificent mansion next door to Dick Clark, who had been the host of *American Bandstand* for a few decades. In front of Mr. Gordy's home, Maria felt she'd faint. She could barely hold up her camera to snap a few photos of the sprawling mansion that was near a beach. Her hands shook, and Greg laughed at the sight of Maria's nervousness. He knew that she had always felt great admiration toward Berry Gordy.

He decided they should dine in Malibu, and he drove into the commercial district to Indie's Restaurant, a seafood diner. He parked near the diner, and they went inside and were seated. A waitress handed them their menus.

"So, you have taken a lot of great photos," Greg said as they opened their menus.

Maria smiled. She was still in awe of having been so close to Berry Gordy's home that she found it hard to sit back and relax. It was mesmerizing to realize how Mr. Gordy's life had been on an upward trajectory since the early 1960s. She felt he was amazing.

"Yes, I did take some great shots, Greg, and thank you for showing me all these wonderful sights. I mean, your home, Berry's, and all the artists' homes are just breathtaking."

"Well, a home is where love is shared," Greg commented, "and I am looking for a special lady to share my home with me."

Maria felt startled by Greg's comment, and not knowing how to respond, she was grateful that the waitress walked up to take their order. Greg ordered red snapper with red skins and asparagus, and Maria ordered whitefish with mixed vegetables. Greg also ordered white wine. The waitress left their table.

"You seemed surprised when I said I'd like to share my home with a special lady," Greg commented.

"Yes, well," Maria began, "I remember when you said that you planned to return to Detroit, that you don't care to travel forever."

The muscles in Greg's face tightened as he reflected on how he intended to lure Maria much closer to him. He wanted her to know that he needed a special lady in his life.

"That's true," he said and picked up a glass and took a sip of water, "but I will be traveling for about five more years before I return to Detroit; that would not prevent me from enjoying a special relationship with someone."

"Such as a live-in companion?" Maria inquired.

"Yes," Greg replied. "If you really care about someone, you would want to keep them close to you."

CHAPTER 33

The waitress walked up and set down their wine, and they both reached for their glass of wine and took a sip as the waitress walked away. Things were heating up a bit, and they were both on edge—Maria wondering just how far should she go in relating to Greg, and Greg hoping to push Maria over the edge so she would fall into his arms. He needed a nice lady in his life, someone trustworthy, and he was aware how much Maria admired him. He wanted much more than just admiration.

They nervously stared at each other for a while, not sure how to continue their conversation but finding it impossible to dismiss the idea of their being together. Maria knew she could never leave David. He was her pillar and rock, her solid foundation in life. And he was more than that. He was a man she loved and trusted, and she promised she would be by his side throughout life.

Despite all of that, Greg Richmond was the greatest temptation she had ever faced in life. She was fascinated by the life of a celebrity, perhaps not by the travel and sacrifices they had to make but certainly by all the beauty and excitement they enjoyed. She had a sweet and loving family—a good husband, a caring and intelligent son, a wonderful daughter-in-law, and beautiful grandchildren—and she couldn't ask for anything any better, yet here she was in California, fulfilling her wildest dreams, enjoying life with a celebrity. It wasn't only too good to be true, but it was at the core of one of her greatest desires in life: to be able to share in the delights of celebrity life.

Their silence was broken when the waitress returned and set down their dinners. She asked them if they needed anything else, and they both answered no. She then left.

They stared at their food, realizing they had more on their plates than just tasteful food, but they were thinking very deeply about each other. They began eating.

"I have to admit, Maria," Greg said, "that I am deeply attracted to you."

"But you realize I'm married," Maria quickly responded.

Greg took his time in responding. He didn't want to come on like some senseless, greedy person who was also vainglorious and didn't care about others. Although he was setting a trap for a somewhat gullible lady to fall into, he needed to do so with tact.

"I appreciate the fact that you have obligations," Greg went on as they enjoyed their meals, "but we have always wanted to get to know each other and, if possible, be able to share a few pleasures together."

Maria felt warm all over. *Maybe Greg just likes women,* she thought. *Maybe he plans to play the field for a while and he's welcoming me to enjoy his world with him. I don't think it's wrong of him to want to enjoy his life. Life is short,* she reasoned, *and I don't think I've ever had this much fun in my life. Even though I'm not able to become Greg's live-in mate, I wouldn't mind seeing him a few more times. I've come this far in realizing my dreams, and I shouldn't run away from them, but I have to pursue them cautiously.*

"I am very dedicated to David," Maria finally responded. "We've been together for a lot of years, and we have a lovely home and a son who has a beautiful family. I love my son and his wife and my grandchildren, and I am—"

"I don't expect you to end your marriage and move in with me," Greg sharply interrupted, "but there's no reason why we shouldn't keep in touch with each other. You might want to come back here to LA during the first week in December. My band will perform at the Coastal Edge Lounge in Hollywood. We're scheduled for two performances, and afterward, the owner of the lounge is throwing a party at his home in Hollywood Hills. I know you would enjoy that party, and this will be a good way for you to share my world with me. You will be able to decide if you'd like to be a part of my life." They were nearly finished with their meals. "You don't have to rush into anything. I am here for you now and for the months ahead of us."

Maria blushed. Greg's warm and endearing invitation to join him in his world was indeed a special offer; really, it seemed too good to be true, and she liked the fact that he wasn't pressuring her.

"I would really love to see your performance at the Coastal Edge Lounge," she said, feeling excited about it. "And I know that party will be fabulous."

"Call me next month and let me know that you're coming in December, and I'll meet you at the airport."

"Okay. I'll do that."

In a few minutes, they finished dining, and Greg paid the waitress before they departed.

CHAPTER 34

Nelson felt fidgety. He had been sitting in the lobby since four forty-five, and it was now a quarter past six, yet he had not seen Greg or Maria. He had called Maria's room at four thirty, but she did not answer, and so he knew she was out. He was wearing his disguise, the navy cap and sunglasses, which made him feel comfortable as he pursued his job in spying, and he was anxious to film as many photos of Greg and Maria as possible. He hoped she had not gone out to meet her girlfriends again. He was on pins and needles, hoping to capture Maria in a compromising position with Greg. He resented how much confidence and ease Greg displayed in pursuing Maria, a married woman—and not just some married woman, but one who was supposedly devoted to his best friend.

He glanced his watch. It was now twenty minutes past six, and he felt he couldn't sit much longer; it was boring the life out of him, and he was anxious to get out and find a nice bar and have a jolly good time mixing with a crowd. Just at that moment when he felt he had to relinquish his spy game, Greg and Maria walked into the lobby. They looked good as a couple, and Nelson wondered if Maria would continue to fortify a barrier between the two of them. He carefully followed them up to the twelfth floor, having taken the elevator next to theirs. They exited their elevator a few seconds before he stepped off his, and he slowly walked up to the hallway leading to Maria's room. He noticed them talking, and then Greg pulled Maria close to him and planted a powerful kiss on her. He quickly snapped two photos and then made a mad dash to the stairs. He could not afford to wait for an elevator and chance being seen by Greg; it would have greatly aroused Greg's suspicions as to why he was running into him a second time. He walked down the stairs to the seventh floor and went to his room.

Inside his room, he tossed his cap and sunglasses onto the dresser and pulled his camera from his pants pocket and laid it on the dresser, feeling like some spy who was working for the CIA, rather than an old colleague to a close friend who was like a brother to him. He was beginning to feel like an eccentric old man, but the fact that he was capturing Maria in very convincing displays of her passion toward Greg was giving him great delight. He was now certain that Maria was indeed pursuing a secret affair with this Greg Richmond character, a charismatic musician who was leading her astray from her husband.

He went into the bathroom and gargled, combed his hair, and then left his room to go out and enjoy the nightlife in sunny Universal City.

The next day, Maria's friends picked her up from the hotel, and they went shopping in Beverly Hills. It was exciting for Maria to see a few well-known stars in casual clothes, out shopping and pushing their little ones in strollers. She tried to imagine living near Beverly Hills and being able to mix with so many beautiful people on a regular basis.

After a few hours of shopping in exclusive stores and purchasing a garment made by a prominent designer, the ladies had lunch together, laughed and talked about all the fun things that had happened at Motown when it was a budding company. Maria was tempted to tell them how she had spent several days with Greg Richmond, but they would have bombarded her with questions, and she couldn't afford for them to gossip about her and Greg when she was still married to David. She was dying to reveal her secret but had to resist all the urges in order to protect her marriage.

Later in the day, when she returned to the hotel shortly before six, Nelson felt stiff as a board as he stared at her. *Oh, she went on some type of shopping spree,* he groaned within himself. Maria vanished from the lobby, and Nelson left the hotel and went to dinner at a restaurant that was in the heart of the action in Universal City.

CHAPTER 35

The following morning, Nelson showered and dressed by seven and went to a small café in the lobby of the hotel for breakfast. He wasn't sure when Maria might check out of the hotel, but he guessed that she had probably scheduled her shopping spree at the tail end of her vacation.

He ate a quick breakfast, and by seven forty-five, he was back on duty in the lobby, hopefully to wrap up his spy work. He put on his cap and sunglasses and purchased a *Wall Street Journal*. He sat in the lobby and read the paper for nearly an hour before Greg Richmond walked in. For the first time since he had been spying on him and Maria, he noticed Greg was dressed in jeans and a light-blue polo shirt and tennis shoes. He had a strong feeling that he would be taking Maria to the airport. She couldn't stay in LA forever, he reasoned, even though God knows she certainly found a lot to do. He couldn't stand another day of trying to keep up with her. Fifteen minutes later, Greg and Maria appeared in the lobby; Greg was carrying her suitcase, and she was carrying her wardrobe bag. Maria checked out at the desk, and they left the lobby for the valet parking garage.

Nelson folded his newspaper and began walking toward the entrance. He walked three blocks to a drugstore and have the film in his throwaway camera developed, and he would pick up the photos near the end of the day. He would have the pictures enlarged one size, so that Maria and Greg's features would be clearly distinguishable. He didn't want David to have any doubts as to what he was up against—a handsome, wealthy, world-famous trumpeter who was romancing his wife.

In two days, Nelson would be back in the suburbs of Detroit, in his four-bedroom ranch home, with his wife in Dearborn Heights. He would keep his photos concealed from his wife in a desk drawer in his office in their basement until he was ready to show them to David. He felt he should hang on to the photos until after Thanksgiving and Christmas, because he didn't want to spoil the holidays for David and his family.

After landing at the airport in Detroit, Maria secured her bags, and then went to the front of the terminal and got in a taxi that took her home. She was very happy and thrilled over her stay in LA and felt she had acquired memories that would last her a lifetime. When she returned to LA in December to see Greg perform at a nightclub in Hollywood, and to attend a party in Hollywood Hills, that would certainly put the icing on the cake. She would have fulfilled her wildest dreams by sharing in the lifestyle of the rich and famous.

That evening, David returned home from work at the university at six, and Maria raced to the door to greet him. He was very happy to see her and glad that she had made it home safely. He ordered dinner for them from a Chinese restaurant, and while they ate in their dining room, Maria related to David all the many wonderful sights she had seen in LA, and when they retired to their bedroom, she would let him see the photos she had taken during her trip. She told him he would be blown away to see the mansions that Berry Gordy and Motown artists owned in the suburbs of Los Angeles. David told her he would love to see those photos, and that he was glad she had a great trip. Maria felt she should wait a couple of days before telling David that she planned to return to California in December to attend a concert and an after party in Hollywood Hills.

CHAPTER 36

The following weekend, David and Maria were heading to a Hallmark Store where Maria chose to buy her Christmas cards every year, and she would choose a couple of gifts for Jonathan and Nicole. Later, she and David would go to Toys R Us and pick out gifts for their grandchildren. They were very excited about seeing them on December 22 and having them in their home for five days. Maria knew she'd go absolutely crazy over their grandchildren.

David slowly drove north on Woodward Avenue toward Nine Mile Road, where they would shop at Hallmark in the city of Royal Oak.

"Sweetheart, I'm taking a group of students to South Dakota to visit Mount Rushmore during the first week in December. They're excited about going because it will be a special treat for them before Christmas, and really, it will be like a wonderful holiday vacation for them. I'd hate to be away from you, but when I return, we'll enjoy preparing for our visit from Jonathan and his family," David said as he drove down Woodward.

Maria's face glowed as she thought about how perfect it was that David would be away during the first week of December, and that he certainly couldn't object to her spending a few days in LA while he was away.

"That will be a wonderful trip for you and your students, David," Maria responded, "and my friends in LA have invited me to attend a concert with them and also a preholiday party in Hollywood Hills. I told them I didn't think you'd mind."

"No, not at all, but are you sure you want to make another trip to LA so soon after your vacation there?"

"I'd love it, David. I will be gone for only four days, and you will be in South Dakota, so we'll both enjoy a bit of excitement before Christmas."

"Yes, that's true. So, will you return to the same hotel in LA?"

"Most definitely. I enjoyed staying there, and as I said, it's only for four days."

David pulled into a parking space near the Hallmark Store and parked his car. He wondered for a few moments if Maria was becoming attracted to LA and perhaps wished she lived there. Maybe she was beginning to feel bored with her suburban life in Detroit. But he dismissed his thoughts. He felt that she simply needed to experience more of life while she was still relatively young, and he couldn't blame her for wanting to get away for a few days to share a bit of excitement with her friends. He had traveled quite a bit, and he knew it would be selfish of him to deprive her of a chance to travel also and enjoy a few special events in life. He didn't want her to feel like a prisoner in her home, as if she were there merely to cook and clean and make him happy. He wanted her to have an enriched life like his own.

"I could tell by the photos that you took in so many beautiful areas in LA, around beaches and valleys, that you had a great time there and that you were glad to be with old friends," David said as they walked toward the store.

"Yes, we had a wonderful time, and this concert we'll attend in December will feature musicians who used to work for Motown. It will be a lot of fun for us to enjoy ourselves before the holiday."

David smiled as he opened the door to the store. "I'm glad you'll be able to enjoy yourself for a few days. We'll both be back home in time to prepare for a visit with Jonathan and his family, and we'll have time to enjoy each other before they arrive."

"That's so true," Maria said, and they began browsing through the store.

CHAPTER 37

In the fall, Maria always felt that the holidays came in rapid succession, and they were big events. Halloween seemed to have been growing out of proportion and was almost a consummate holiday. Halloween decorations were nearly as plentiful as Christmas decorations. Thanksgiving seemed sandwiched between Halloween and Christmas and losing quite a bit of its appeal. Nevertheless, Maria and David made sure they enjoyed a special dinner on Thanksgiving with friends or distant relatives, and they especially enjoyed visiting a museum. They both enjoyed delighting in the past and viewing all of the inventions that had been created over the centuries. This Thanksgiving, they would visit the Henry Ford Museum in Dearborn, Michigan, which they hadn't visited in a number of years. They loved seeing the old cars and trains that were on display at the museum and experiencing the otherworldly environment at the museum that romanced their spirits.

In early November, Maria scheduled her flight to Los Angeles and booked a room at the Hilton in Universal City. She also phoned Greg and related to him the time and date she would arrive at the airport in LA. He agreed to meet her inside the terminal at the Delta Airlines ticket counter, just as they had met on her previous trip.

Maria regarded Greg Richmond as her special friend and in no other way. She would never leave David for him. David was her knight in shining armor. He had brought her out of the darkness when she was alone on Wayne State's campus, feeling minuscule compared to the sea of students surrounding her. They embraced each other, overlooking their weaknesses and providing each other with courage and strength. They had grown together over the years and had become more confident people. They also had a wonderful son, daughter-in-law, and grandchildren, and for these reasons, their lives had become rich. Her family represented her true richness and greatness in life. She did not feel that Greg Richmond cared anything about her family life. He was so fixated on himself and his success that he had not ever expressed any admiration of the fine way she led her life.

Despite the way Greg was centered on himself and his accomplishments in life, he was her key to being able to experience the lifestyle of the rich and famous. He was the avenue to her dreams, and she would be able to enjoy that celebrity life, if only for a short while.

On December 5, David departed early that morning and headed to the airport, where he would meet his students, and they would fly to South Dakota to view Mount Rushmore. The next day, Maria left home and drove to the airport to catch her early-morning flight to Los Angeles. Both she and David would return home a few days later on a Sunday evening.

When Maria arrived in Los Angeles on that Wednesday afternoon, Greg promptly met her at the Delta Airlines ticket counter inside the terminal, and minutes later, they were in his Bentley as he drove to the Hilton Hotel in Universal City. Maria was thrilled to be back in Los Angeles and to have an opportunity to see Greg perform at the Coastal Edge Lounge. Greg was just as thrilled at being with Maria, feeling he was succeeding in drawing her closer to him.

Once they arrived at the Hilton, Maria checked in, and Greg escorted her to her room, where she put her luggage away. Then they went to the diner on the first floor of the hotel and ordered dinner.

As they dined, Greg told Maria that he had band rehearsal the next day, and that evening, his son, Antonio, and his family were coming to his home at five o'clock to have dinner with him. He said he needed to take time from his busy schedule to spend time with his son and his family. He asked Maria what her plans were for the next day, and she told him she really wanted to spend the day shopping in Universal City, that a number of stores had attracted her. He told her that was a good idea and that he hoped she would enjoy her day. He added that he would greet her at the Coastal Edge that Friday if she got there by eight thirty, a half hour before the show started, and she agreed to do so.

After dinner, Greg rode on the elevator with Maria to her room on the eighth floor, and he warmly kissed her good night at the door. She had made it clear to him that she wished to keep her relationship with him strictly on a friendship level, and so he never tried to force himself on her and never insisted on visiting her in her room. He felt that after seeing him perform at the lounge, she would definitely want to be with him after the show and the party in the Hills.

Greg departed, and Maria went inside her room, showered, and dressed for bed. In an instant, she was fast asleep.

The next day, she spent several hours shopping in Universal City and bought herself several beautiful gifts. She wanted to always remember the special times she spent in sunny California and how much she enjoyed the warmth and beauty all around her, and especially how Greg had helped her to see the way in which Motown's artists lived in LA.

CHAPTER 38

On Friday evening, Maria dressed in a deep-blue sequined sleeveless dress and a black satin jacket. She wore small diamond earrings and let her lovely silky black hair flow over her shoulders. She wore black satin shoes and carried a matching evening bag. At eight o'clock, she stepped out front of the Hilton and got into a cab. The driver drove her to the Coastal Edge Lounge, which was nearly a half hour away. She paid the cab driver, walked up to the door of the lounge, and gave the doorman forty dollars, which was the price of admission. After she walked inside, almost immediately, Greg walked up to her, smiling brilliantly.

"Maria! Wow, you look gorgeous!" he exclaimed. He knew for certain that she would be in his arms at the end of the night.

"Thank you, Greg."

"I saved you a seat up front with two of our friends, Sheila and Gloria. They have been attending our concerts for a few years. You can ride to the after party with them."

"Okay, that's fine with me," Maria said.

"Come on, I'll introduce you to them."

Maria followed Greg through the crowded lounge to a table where two white women sat. They both looked to have been in their midthirties. Maria felt that they were like so many white women in the country who idolized black men, but she felt that she could endure them for one night.

Standing before the women, Greg made introductions, and then he told Maria he would see her at the after party, and he quickly departed.

Maria eased into a seat, and the women smiled at her.

"Greg told us you used to work for Motown," Sheila said.

"Yes," Maria responded, "and that was really a long time ago."

The women laughed. A waitress popped up, and Maria ordered a margarita. The women were both drinking scotch.

"Did you enjoy your flight?" Gloria asked. She was a blonde like her friend, but a bit heavier. Both women were pleasant looking.

"Yes, I did," Maria said. "It was very smooth."

The waitress walked up and set down Maria's drink, and Maria paid her. She didn't intend on running a tab.

"We've been following Greg's band for a few years," Sheila explained. "We're both divorced, and it gives us something to do." The women sipped their drinks for a few seconds, and then Sheila inquired, "Are you also divorced?"

"No," Maria quietly responded, and the women looked at each other very briefly, taking in Maria's status and realizing she would not be a groupie. They wondered if she had a thing for Greg.

"A lot of women go wild over Greg!" Gloria spat out her words in a slurred tone, and Maria wondered how many drinks they'd had.

"I'm happily married," Maria said. "I simply love to travel, and Greg invited me here to see his show."

Sheila and Gloria laughed.

"Yes, well, Gloria and I were happily married once," Sheila said, "but after a couple of kids and seven or eight years of arguing over bills, you start tipping around, and then you land in divorce court."

Maria looked around the spacious lounge that could seat two hundred people; nearly every seat was filled. The majority of the people seemed to have been in their thirties and forties, with a few older and younger people. Maria realized that Greg Richmond and the Soul Invaders' soul-jazz music greatly appealed to young professionals.

CHAPTER 39

Soon, a tall, slender black man was on the stage and at the mike. "Hey, out there!" he said in a jovial tone. "I'm Tony Bell, as most of you know, the DJ here at the Edge, and I must say that all of you are looking fantastic tonight." He paused for a moment and glanced over the crowd. "Yes, indeed, there are quite a few foxes in the audience." Everyone laughed. "And don't hesitate to get up and dance if the music grooves you, and I know it certainly will. You're going to want to swing those hips!" Tony swayed back and forth, and there was more laughter. "Because you know Greg Richmond and the Soul Invaders can really get down. Okay, so now, let's give it up for Greg Richmond and the Soul Invaders!" Everyone began clapping as Greg and his band walked out on the stage.

Greg went to the mike. "Hello, everyone," he said in a deep, soft voice.

"Greg! Greg!" a woman shouted out. "You've got it going on, baby!" Everyone laughed.

"It's good seeing all of you," Greg went on. "It's always a pleasure to be with you here in LA. You have been our loyal followers for many years, and we certainly appreciate you. In a few weeks, we will be on the East Coast in New York, in the deep freeze, joining in on Christmas and New Year's celebrations. Right now, we're going to play for you 'Sangria.'"

Greg and his band began playing a jazzy, slightly Spanish tune, and as Greg pumped away on his trumpet, several people jumped up and raced to the dance floor and danced away, swaying and rocking to the music. Greg's pecan-brown skin glowed under the stage lights, and his dark brows furrowed as he blew his horn from the depth of his soul.

Maria, and Greg's friends who sat with her, gently rocked in their seats, and Maria's heart was ignited with deep admiration toward her favorite musician, who had developed his skills at Motown in the old days. He was now like a rocket, exploding on the world scene. The tune, "Sangria," lasted long enough for the dancers to feel nearly exhausted, and when it ended, they scurried back to their seats.

The band then began playing "Blue Velvet Nights," and several couples went onto the dance floor and held each other tight as they glided along to the warm, sensual music. The band played long versions of each tune, allowing everyone to savor the moments. Once "Blue Velvet Nights" ended, they proceeded to play a succession of hit recordings, such as "Shining Wheels," "Embrace the Magic," "Early Morning Love," and "Lost in the Rain."

After the band's performance, there was a forty-minute intermission before the next show began. Maria, Gloria, and Sheila rushed to use the ladies' room, and then, when they returned, they ordered a large nachos and Cokes. They were having a wonderful night out among lively partygoers, and they anticipated even more fun at the after party in Hollywood Hills.

The second show started out with Greg and the Soul Invaders playing "Heat Wave." Three handsome Mexican guys walked up to Maria, Gloria, and Sheila, and led them out on the dance floor. They danced away and were having great fun and enjoyment. The men kept them on the dance floor for the next number, "Grazing in the Grass." Greg had decided that his band should play a few of the old favorite tunes that had been quite popular. They went on to play a half dozen of their soul-jazz hits.

CHAPTER 40

By the end of the second show at half past midnight, Maria felt very comfortable being with Gloria and Sheila. She had learned that Gloria was a physical education teacher at an elementary school, and Sheila worked for Newpointe Advertising as an art director. They had lived near each other in the valley since they were young children. Maria informed them that after she left Motown, she began a career at Wayne State University as a supervisor in admissions.

The women were eager to party in the Hills. Sheila jumped into her Corvette, and Gloria and Maria got into Gloria's Lexus, and they sped out of the parking lot of the Coastal Edge and dashed onto the freeway. In twenty-two minutes, they were cruising through the hills at the very top, among dozens of colossal mansions, until they got to a well-lit, light-gray mansion, with the drapes and blinds open over several windows and a long, wide driveway that was filled with cars. Gloria and Sheila parked on the street in front of the mansion, realizing it might take a while for them to get out of the driveway once they were ready to leave. They told Maria that they would party for a couple of hours and that they knew Greg would take her to her hotel once she was ready to leave. Maria had butterflies in her stomach. She had never been to a party in such an elaborate mansion, and she hoped it wouldn't take Greg too long before he arrived.

When the three ladies walked up on the expansive porch, the homeowner, Bert George, who also owned the Coastal Edge, greeted them as he stood before the front door. He was about five feet five in height and was quite thin, with receding black hair and was wearing a bright smile.

"Ladies, welcome to my home," he said.

"Thank you, Mr. George," Gloria replied. "We just left the Coastal Edge and had a magnificent time."

"I'm glad you did. Are you guests of Mr. Greg Richmond?"

"Yes, we are," Sheila replied.

"Very well. Welcome to the party."

Gloria, Sheila, and Maria walked inside the very spacious home, with plush, light-tan carpeting throughout the first floor and handsome Italian sofas and chairs in the living room and a few small Italian chairs in the hallway. There was a brilliant chandelier above the very long dining room table, and more than fifty guests were scattered throughout the house. Piped-in music filled the home, and Maria recognized the voices of the Bee Gees as they poured out a warm and tender song. She stood alongside of Gloria and Sheila in the living room, where they decided to remain until Maria could connect with Greg. A tall, handsome Italian man walked into the living room, carrying a tray of hors d'oeuvres, and the ladies grabbed a few. The servant told them that drinks were served at the back of the hallway in the family room. Just as he departed, Greg entered the living room with his arm around a lovely Spanish lady in a black silk dress with a plunging neckline. Maria gazed at Greg in shock.

"Oh, that's that damn Nicki Rowe," Sheila told Maria. "She's a makeup artist at channel 24, and she was lucky enough to marry the producer of the *Late Show*. Her marriage only lasted a few years. The producer found out she's bisexual, and she also has a thing for black men."

Greg whispered to Nicki that he had to talk with an old friend, and she kissed him on the lips and headed toward the back to get a drink. Just as Greg began walking toward Maria, a beautiful blonde with long, straight hair, who was dressed in a pink silk minidress walked up to Greg and kissed him on the lips. They began talking.

"That's Candy Sims," Gloria said. "She's a fashion designer, and she owns a boutique called Candy's Corner. She also has the hots for musicians, and I don't know who is more notorious, her or Nicki."

Greg talked with Candy for a few minutes, and then he finally walked up to Gloria, Sheila, and Maria. Maria felt completely startled by the women who were throwing themselves at Greg, and she realized how cool and comfortably he reacted toward it. She couldn't imagine herself being married to someone who attracted so many different women.

CHAPTER 41

"**L**adies, it's good to see you," Greg said.

We're his fans, Maria thought. *This house is filled with women who are anxious to see him.* Just then, the Commodores' record came on, and they belted out a song about a woman being a brick house, and two women rushed up to Greg and said, "Greg, you promised to have a drink with us." They grabbed him and led him to the family room. Maria felt dazed.

"Well, let's go into the family room," Sheila said. The ladies walked down the hallway past several people who were drinking and talking with each other. The home was full of people, and the music, food, and drinks were unending. The family room was filled with a lively crowd. Maria noticed Greg was surrounded by six women; two were very beautiful African American women. Maria realized that Bert George was throwing this party for Greg and his band members, since they were so popular in LA, and the Coastal Edge always had sellout crowds whenever they performed there. What she failed to consider was that there were many women who were eager to get to Greg, and he would have very little time to spend with her at this party.

"I have to use the restroom," she told Sheila.

"There's one down the hall, and if it's occupied, you can use the one upstairs," Sheila said.

"Thanks."

Maria raced down the hall and knocked on a closed door.

"This one is taken!" a lady yelled out.

She then raced farther down the hall to the spiral stairwell, with maple steps and brass banister, and she walked to the second level of the home. She noticed there were five rooms on this floor. She walked down the hall. The door to the first room was open, and she peered in and noticed two of Greg's band members and three other men sniffing cocaine from a round glass table. The band members' eyes became as big as two moons when they noticed Maria staring at them. She quietly moved on. The door to the next room was also open, and Maria noticed six people in there. Three were totally knocked out on a sofa, looking dazed, and as if they were drifting off the planet. One man had a syringe tightly wrapped around his arm, and he was injecting heroin into his vein. Two other men were intently staring at him as if they were eager for their turn. Maria began looking pale, and she could feel her body trembling. She walked a bit farther down the hall, and this time the door to a room was closed. She could hear what sounded like three women talking and laughing, and a man said, "This is going to be one fantastic night!" Maria realized they were having an orgy. Across the hall, the bathroom door was open, and she rushed in, locked the door, and quickly used the bathroom. She washed her hands, thinking, *This celebrity life is not for me!*

Once she was back on the first floor and in the family room, Maria noticed Greg surrounded by more people, and they were in uproarious laughter. Maria walked over to Gloria and said, "I'd like to leave, Gloria. I'll never get a chance to talk with Greg."

"Okay," Gloria said, while listening to Greg entertaining his friends about some of his encounters with people in other countries. "We can leave in a half hour. I'm very tired."

"I'll be in the living room," Maria replied.

"Okay, fine. I'll see you in a little while."

Maria walked to the living room, passing people in the hallway who were drinking and chatting. Natalie Cole's sweet voice was pouring through the house in a song about an everlasting love. The living room was filled with people who were dressed in jazzy partygoing styles. Maria found an empty chair near the huge picture window, and she sat down and stared out the window into the darkness. The well-lit front porch allowed her to see to the end of the driveway. Fancy cars were lined up all around the house. Maria sat and thought about how the celebrity life wasn't meant for her. She would never get used to drugs, wild sex, and the constant fast pace of a celebrity's life. She enjoyed sharing in the luxuries and the special events surrounding a celebrity, but she realized there were too many dangerous pitfalls embedded in their lifestyle and that she could not live in their world.

"Hello," Gloria said, and Maria nearly jumped out of her seat. Gloria laughed. "We can go."

Maria blushed, realizing how she had been lost in thought. She followed Gloria outside to her car.

Inside Gloria's Lexus, as they sailed along the freeway toward the Hilton Hotel, Maria realized she did not regret not having an opportunity to talk with Greg at the party.

"I know you were disappointed that you weren't able to talk with Greg," Gloria said as she swiftly drove along in light, fast-moving traffic.

"No, I realize how popular he is," Maria said. "It's been a wonderful weekend. I have no regrets."

"It's good you had a chance to see what Greg's life is like. I'm sure you wouldn't want to leave your husband for him."

"No, never," Maria firmly replied. She had never considered leaving David, and now she was satisfied in knowing that a life in the entertainment world would not be suitable for her. She wouldn't be able to cope with crowds, eccentric behavior, or constant travel. Her fantasies and curiosities were over.

Soon, Gloria pulled up in front of the Hilton Hotel, and she and Maria commented on the fun they had shared. Gloria wished Maria a safe return home, and Maria thanked her and departed her car, and headed inside the hotel.

CHAPTER 42

That next morning, the sharp ringing of Maria's telephone awakened her. Groggy, Maria stared at the small clock on an end table next to her bed and noticed it was eleven in the morning. She picked up. "Hello."

"Well, what a great night we had," Greg's voice boomed into Maria's ears. She sat up in bed, startled. "You fly all the way here from Detroit and then leave the party when it was just getting started."

Maria couldn't believe her ears. Greg was scolding her for having left the party, but while she was there, he had not exchanged five words with her.

"I didn't think you'd notice," she said.

"How long do you plan to keep avoiding me?"

"I was tired, and it was quite late, and so—"

Greg slammed down his receiver, and Maria could feel her heart pounding against her chest. Now she had to reckon with the fact that underneath Greg's cool exterior was an impatient and cold side to him that she had never cared to know about or experience. She also knew she had merely been chasing a dream, and the dream was over. She knew for certain that she did not belong in Greg's world.

The day seemed to have lasted forever. She got out of bed, showered, and went to the first floor of the hotel to have a late breakfast in a small café. Afterward, she walked around in Universal City, window shopping for a while, and then decided to make a few purchases on her last day there. Later, she dined in a restaurant near the Hilton, and after dinner, she returned to her hotel room, undressed, and slipped on a nightshirt. She turned on the TV and stared at the images on the screen. It was a travel program, and it seemed as if the host was walking down a street in Italy or Greece; it was not clear to her where the host may have been. All she could think about was how Greg had slammed the phone in her face. He wasn't even a decent friend, so there was no way she could have become close to him, and she had told him from the start that she was dedicated to her husband.

After sitting idly in her bed, staring at scenes in a foreign country, she turned off the television, set an alarm for eight in the morning, and soon fell fast asleep.

The next morning, she sprang to life and briskly dashed about, washing up, dressing, and packing to leave for the airport by nine thirty. She would catch a Delta flight to Detroit at twelve forty-five, and she would happily drive herself home from the airport. She was glad that her visit to another kingdom in California had come to an end. She was anxious to return to her normal, routine way of life.

She looked around her hotel room and was satisfied that she had carefully packed all of her possessions, so she grabbed her luggage and wardrobe bag and quickly left the room.

CHAPTER 43

S oon she was on a shuttle bus with four other people, heading to the airport. The driver aggressively maneuvered through traffic, having to slow down numerous times, and even coming to a halt, but once freed from tight spots, the driver continued on. After nearly two hours, Maria safely arrived at the airport, along with the other passengers.

She deposited her bags with a baggage attendant and found her way to gate H14, where she sat and waited for the flight back to Detroit. She was happy to leave behind her search and conquest of her greatest dreams, to share in the life of a celebrity; it had been a bittersweet dream, and she was all too happy to return home.

Soon she was buckled into her seat on a Delta plane, and in no time, she was sailing through the skies. It was a wonderful feeling to have a lovely home and a great husband to return home to, rather than wandering around among strangers and feeling empty inside. Perhaps she needed this adventure to help her appreciate the simpler and more precious things in life, such as love, caring, and trust—everything she had in David. She relaxed on her journey home and thought about how good it would feel to be in David's arms. She also thought about the sweetness and beauty of life. Her son and his family would soon be at her home, and she couldn't wait to behold them. The joy she shared with her family was more special than anything in the world. It had been a pleasure for her to view the other side of Motown and to know how Motown's artists continued to prosper for many years after the company had been sold. She loved viewing their gorgeous mansions, but she also knew that every home and every heart is blessed by their faith in God. Material things, and even life itself may pass away, but God's love is eternal.

After a safe flight home, Maria secured her baggage and went to her car in the airport parking lot. She threw her bags in the back seat of the car and drove home. At home, David opened the door for her, and she put down her bags. They embraced, united in a warm, long kiss. After Maria settled in, she and David enjoyed the dinner he had prepared of sirloin steak, rice pilaf, and broccoli. They enjoyed relating their experiences in South Dakota and California; it had been refreshing for both of them to have taken a short vacation before Christmas. That night, they enjoyed warm, intense lovemaking, and their hearts were filled with ecstasy.

CHAPTER 44

On December 22, Jonathan, Nicole, and their three children arrived at David and Maria's home in the late afternoon. When they rang the doorbell, David and Maria rushed to the door and greeted them. They were overjoyed to see how fine they looked, and Maria helped her grandchildren remove their winter coats. Her grandsons, Shelton and Aiden, were growing strong like their father, and the baby girl, Julie, was taking steady steps in walking for a two-year-old. They all went into the living room, where David and Maria had decorated a small tree, and placed gifts under it. They excitedly talked about traveling from one continent to another and how to keep children occupied during a long flight. Shelton and Aiden were anxious to tell their grandparents about what they were learning in school and how they wanted to build houses on the island when they grew up. Jonathan said they had watched builders developing houses near their home, and they became fascinated with the trade.

Julie began singing "Jingle Bells," and everyone laughed. Nicole said that Julie loved watching morning programs for children on TV, and she had just learned how to sing a couple of songs. Nicole talked about how her parents were doing fine and that her mother enjoyed taking care of the children while she and Jonathan were at work.

David said that after breakfast the next day, they would ride around Belle Isle to see the marvelous winter wonderland and the beauty of ice-covered trees and frozen ponds, and the children could play in the snow. They were excited about being able to enjoy all the snow and ice, which they had never seen in Hawaii.

After conversing for nearly two hours, everyone dressed for bed and slept soundly during the night.

The next day, they all went riding in Jonathan's rented Edge SUV to Belle Isle, an island park, where thick icicles hung from trees and wind-blown snow was stacked in piles. The children had a joyful time in the snow and sliding across slippery ponds. David helped them to make a small snowman, and Jonathan led them close to a pond filled with ducks. He explained to them that the ducks were able to keep warm on the ice due to the oil in their bodies. Nicole and Maria noticed a small wooden café, and so, before leaving the island, they stopped and bought hot chocolate and drank it before leaving the park.

On the way home, they stopped at an International House of Pancakes, and everyone ate a big breakfast, enjoying their choice of pancakes. David and Maria felt so much happiness being close to their grandchildren and delighting in how they were growing up in a fine manner, having gentle natures and loving hearts. They realized what a fine job Jonathan and Nicole were doing in raising their grandchildren.

When they returned home, the children ran all over the house, and Nicole chased behind them and made sure they did not destroy anything in the house. Maria told her not to worry because she and David had put anyway anything that might cause the children harm or that might be easily broken.

While Jonathan and Nicole relaxed in the living room, David and Maria went into the kitchen and prepared a quick dinner, a large meatloaf, mashed potatoes, and mixed vegetables. There would be plenty of food by five o'clock in the evening. After preparing dinner, David and Maria went into the living room, where Jonathan and his family were watching a professional ice skating competition. Maria picked up Julie and hugged her tight, letting her sit in her lap as they watched the skaters. She was immensely happy holding her granddaughter, who stared into her face more than at the TV screen.

CHAPTER 45

On Christmas morning, Nicole and the children opened their gifts, as David and Maria urged them to do. Meanwhile, they began cooking dinner, which they would serve at three o'clock. David prepared a ham and roasted chicken. Maria made the dressing, green beans with white potatoes, and candied yams. Jonathan enjoyed a late-morning sleep, getting caught up on much-needed rest.

Soon, Nicole fixed breakfast for everyone, and they all ate together; Jonathan said a prayer. Maria was so pleased that her son hadn't forgotten how to put God first in their lives, which she had taught him to do when he was a young child and throughout his life. After breakfast, David, Maria, Nicole, and Jonathan opened their gifts and were pleased over the beautiful jewelry they exchanged with each other.

At dinnertime, David said a prayer, and everyone enjoyed a wonderful dinner. Maria took several photos of her family at the dinner table, and she would take several more photos throughout the day.

After dinner, the children played with their toys while David, Maria, Nicole, and Jonathan sat in the den and listened to Christmas songs and drank eggnog with cognac. Maria was in heaven, enjoying her family in such warmth and love. She and David knew in their hearts that they would miss Jonathan and his family a great deal once they departed.

The day after Christmas, David and Maria prepared a large breakfast for everyone, and close to noon, they went to a local theater to see a Disney movie about planet Earth. Nicole and Jonathan loved movies about the Earth, which helped their children to appreciate the kind of work they did as environmentalists. Nicole, Jonathan, and their children attended a Methodist church every Sunday, and Jonathan taught his children to pray to God to bless the Earth, our home.

The two-hour movie was awesome, and the children loved it. Afterward, David treated everyone to lunch at Ponderosa, where there was a large salad bar, filled with a variety of meats, salads, and desserts. It was a special place for many churchgoers to congregate after services. The restaurant was always filled to capacity with a lively crowd.

The days passed quickly, and soon, Jonathan and his family were packing and preparing to head to the airport. David and Maria hugged and kissed them and promised to visit them in a couple of years. Maria held her granddaughter for a while before their departure and gave her tender kisses. David was quite proud of Jonathan for the fine manner in which he was caring for his family. They departed on a snowy, icy day to return to their beloved island.

CHAPTER 46

David and Maria enjoyed warm, passionate lovemaking for several days after Jonathan and his family's departure. They were filled with happiness, and their union was greatly strengthened by family ties. They were also back to their rigorous work routine at the university, David being fully charged in explaining historical events to his students, and Maria in welcoming new students to the Graduate School of Social Work. She and David also enjoyed uniting with their special friends on campus.

One night in mid-January, David and Maria were sound asleep at ten o'clock when their doorbell rang. Maria was so tired that the bell did not disturb her, but David, who was always sharply alert, jumped out of bed, quite annoyed. He put on his robe, slipped into his house shoes, and walked swiftly to the door. He looked out into the night, with a gentle snowfall, and he noticed Nelson Weinstein standing there in a charcoal-gray wool coat and hat. He opened the door.

"Nelson, what a surprise," David said. "Come in. What brings you my way at this hour?"

"I wanted to come while Maria was asleep," Nelson said softly. "I hope she's sleeping."

"Yes, she is," David replied. "Let me take your coat."

Nelson was holding a large brown envelope, and he switched the envelope to his left hand as he eased out of his coat and hat and handed them to David, who immediately hung them up.

"I have very important photos to show you," Nelson said, "and only you. Maria should not see these right now."

"All right, so let's go into the living room."

They went into the living room and sat on the sofa. Nelson took the photos from the envelope and handed David all ten of the pictures. David first looked at four photographs of a man with Maria in front of the door to a hotel room. Then there was a photo of them leaving a parked car in the driveway of a luxurious home. Next was the most offensive photo David had viewed, where the man was kissing Maria's breast as they stood by the side of a pool. There were a few more photos of the man kissing Maria in front of her hotel room.

"Who is this man in these photos?" David snapped, his blood pressure soaring.

"Greg Richmond. He's a famous trumpeter who used to work for Motown Records. Your wife has been having an affair with him."

David became so angry, he felt like ripping the photos to pieces and throwing them into the trash, but he knew he had to calm down. He had to show these photos to Maria and find out what in the hell she was doing behind his back. He could not believe she was cheating on him, and for what reason? They had a good marriage. Was it lust? Was this some man that she had always desired but could not have, and now, was she longing to be with him? David did not know if he could contain his anger through the night, but he would have to calm down and wait until after they came home from work the next day before confronting her.

He took in a deep breath, feeling as if Nelson had dropped a bomb on him. The muscles in his jaws became tight. "Nelson, why did you take these photos?" he demanded. The pictures disgusted him.

Nelson stretched his long legs. "I knew you'd ask me that. I wish I could smoke."

"You'd better not light up one of those damn cigars."

"I said I *wish* I could smoke. Listen, I didn't go to LA in order to spy on Maria. I had to meet with clients, but one evening, I was cruising through Hollywood, and I noticed Maria and this man leaving the Brown Derby, and I followed them. My curiosity got the best of me. I ended up following them for several days, and I took photos of them so that you could see that Maria is having an affair with this character."

David released a heavy sigh. "That explains why she went back to Los Angeles during the first week in December."

"Are you shitting me?"

"No," David replied, sadly shaking his head. "I don't understand her, and I've always felt closer to her than anyone I've known."

"I told you she was bored. I mean, you should have recognized that with Jonathan being away and all the silence in your home. I tried to warn you that she just might go out and look for a bit of excitement."

"A bit of excitement? The woman made two trips to LA, goddamn it; that was more than just a bit of excitement. She's chasing a man and at the same time pretending to be a faithful wife."

"Some people live double lives," Nelson commented.

"Christ, I can't believe how we cooked Christmas dinner together for Jonathan and his family. We had a wonderful Christmas together."

"Yes, well, I hate being the bearer of bad news, but I felt you needed to know the truth about Maria. You know, your mother warned you that these African American women are real sexpots and you can't trust them. I hope you can see that for yourself."

CHAPTER 47

For a moment, David felt like striking Nelson. He could fully sense that Nelson delighted in proving that Maria was worthless based on her race. But wasn't that the same way so many people felt about Jews? Was Nelson trying to force him into those turbulent waters of racial hatred? He stared at Nelson for a long while, wanting to strike him, but the fact that he had to question Maria and find out why she had deceived him far outweighed his desire to knock Nelson flat on his ass.

"Well, you have brought me not only bad news but very shocking news, Nelson, and I have to talk with Maria about what is going on between us."

Nelson rose from the sofa. "It's simple, David. She has hot pants, and you have to decide what you want to do about it." Nelson walked toward the front closet and put on his coat and hat. "I'll call you in a few days. Sorry I had to advise you of such unpleasant matters."

David sat silently as he placed the photos back into the envelope. He was in a state of shock and could not speak. Nelson understood, and he quietly left the home.

The next day, David entered his home at a quarter past six, and he could smell a pleasant aroma from the kitchen. He hung up his hat and coat.

"David, is that you?" Maria called out.

"Yes," he answered in a firm voice. He had the photos Nelson had given him in his leather portfolio. He sat at the dining room table, placing the portfolio on the table. Maria walked into the dining room and gave him a kiss on the cheek.

"I've made vegetable soup," she said.

"I don't care for anything," David replied.

Maria looked puzzled. "Are you okay?"

"Sit down," he said.

Maria felt a chill racing over her. She sat in a chair next to him. He opened the portfolio, took out the photos, and handed them to Maria. She couldn't believe her eyes. There she was, standing in front of her hotel room, and Greg Richmond was kissing her. There were a few more photos of them kissing in front of the door to her hotel room, and they were captured in Greg's backyard, not far from his Bentley. Next, she saw the worst picture she had ever seen in her life! She was captured standing before Greg in a red bikini as he was kissing her breast. She threw the photos onto the dining room table as tears streamed down her face.

"Who on earth took those photos?" she exclaimed.

"Who took them?" David raged. "What difference does it make who took them? That's you in those goddamn photos!" David was infuriated.

"David, someone was trying to incriminate me," Maria cried.

"Incriminate you!" David shouted, the veins in his neck bulging. "You're standing there in front of this man, half-naked, and he's all over your ass, and you say someone was trying to incriminate you!"

"David, please," Maria cried, and she dropped to the floor and hugged him around his leg. "I went to LA to see how the artists that worked for Motown lived, and the man in the photo is just an old friend. He invited me to his home for a swim, and I went, but I didn't expect him to kiss me like that. I pulled up my top, pushed him away, and I went inside his house and put my clothes on and told him to take me back to my hotel. You see," Maria sobbed, "whoever took those photos wanted you to think the worst of me! They didn't photograph the way I left that man's house."

CHAPTER 48

David was even more shocked in learning the truth from Maria. He was certain that Nelson truly wanted him to think the worst of her, but she needed to be taught a lesson. If she thought for one moment that he would allow her to fool around with this musician, she had another thing coming. He wasn't that weak. He would think of a way to punish her.

"Get up off the floor," he said in a strong voice. She rose from the floor, sobbing and wiping her face. "You disgust me," he said, "and I have no idea what you did when you made that second trip to Los Angeles. You said you went to attend a concert, but how can I be certain that that's all you did?" David pushed her hard, and she crashed onto the floor. Fortunately, the floor was carpeted, but her back took a great blow. "Stay away from me!" David demanded, as Maria labored hard to sit up on the floor. "I don't want to sleep with you. I can sleep in the guest room. And I don't want you cooking for me. I can cook my own meals, and I don't want you sitting at the table with me when I'm eating. I'll wash my clothes. I want you to stay the hell away from me. Do you understand?"

"Yes, David," Maria softly cried, and he abruptly left the room. She got up from the floor, staggered over to the dining table, and tore up all the photos. "Some bastard is trying to destroy my marriage!" she cried out in pain.

The next day at work, Maria walked around the admissions office stiffly, with excruciating back pain, but she did not want to take the day off. She had already taken several vacation days. Two of the admissions clerks were noticing her stiff walk, but they were too busy to comment on it. Close to one o'clock, Cynthia Alridge came out of her private office, where she was working on a quarterly budget for the graduate school, and noticed Maria frowning as she bent over a shelf at the front counter and placed a stack of class schedule booklets there. Cynthia walked up to her.

"Are you in pain?" Cynthia asked.

"My back hurts," Maria said in a low voice so that the clerks could not hear her. The clerks were busy transcribing admission interviews that were conducted between the director of admissions and the applicants. "David and I got in a fight, and he pushed me to the floor."

"What?" Cynthia asked in shocked surprise. The thick, brownish-blonde curls in her hair bounced around her head as she stared at Maria in shock. "I can't imagine you and David getting into a fight. Let's go to the American Coney Island in five minutes, so you can tell me what happened."

Soon, Cynthia and Maria were seated in the busy restaurant and had given their orders to a waitress.

"So, what happened between you and David?" Cynthia asked.

"Oh," Maria sighed, "some asshole who knows David was in LA when I made my first trip there, and he took photos of me and Greg Richmond together on several occasions."

Cynthia's hazel eyes popped wide open. "Lord have mercy! You never told me you met with Greg Richmond!"

"It wasn't important, and it wasn't anybody's business."

The waitress walked up, set down the Cokes Cynthia and Maria had ordered, and left.

"Girl, those photos must have been something else! I mean, you're walking around as if you were in a car accident!"

"They weren't that bad. There were several photos of Greg and me standing in front of the door to my hotel room, kissing, and there was a photo of us at his swimming pool at his house."

"And David knocked you to the floor!" Cynthia exclaimed. Her glass shook, and the ice nearly sailed out. "Honestly, he must have seen something in those photos that really upset him. You and David never fight."

"Well," Maria sheepishly began as the waitress walked up and set down their wingding dinners. "I had on this red bikini that Greg bought me, and after we got out of the pool, Greg pulled me close to him and kissed my breast."

Cynthia stared at Maria in shock. She completely forgot about her lunch.

CHAPTER 49

"**G**irl, hum, hum, hum. You went out to LA, chasing that man, and just got yourself into a world of trouble! And some freaking ghost captured everything in photos. Lord, I wondered if you'd let that crush you had on Greg get out of hand."

They began eating.

"Whoever took those photos," Maria said, "is someone who is a close friend to David. David wouldn't say who he is, but it's obviously someone who works here at the university, and they know me. They must have been vacationing in LA at the same time I was, and you know people today will not mind their own business, not even if you paid them. They're all camera happy. I don't know what this world is coming to."

"Were there other people at that pool at Greg's house?"

"No, it was just the two of us."

"You see," Cynthia said, careful not to choke on a wingding, "that's what really got to David; it was just you and Greg at that pool, and why on earth did you let that man kiss your breast?"

"I didn't, Cynthia. I pushed him away from me. I had no idea he was going to do that!"

Cynthia ate her food while she thought for a few moments. "Well, one thing for sure: you knew that man was a hot number; you said so several times. You talked about his sexiness and confidence. He just knew you wanted to sleep with him."

"I made it very clear to him that I would not sleep with him," Maria firmly replied.

"Yeah, but he was looking at you in that swimsuit, and what you said didn't even register."

Maria and Cynthia returned to work, and Maria tried to concentrate on the number of students who needed to take additional prequalifying classes to determine if they would be able to handle a full-time curriculum, but thoughts about the terrible fight she had with David kept blocking her ability to concentrate. She struggled the entire afternoon, examining fifty files and the academic transcripts in each file, as her mind kept drifting from her work. She could only see David yelling at her and pushing her to the floor. She feared how he might react toward her during the days ahead, and she froze in fear of what he might do to her. She was unable to concentrate on her work, barely making it through half of the student files. She would simply start over the next day, after she took time to calm down and put her fears aside.

When she entered her home at five thirty in the evening, she wondered how she was going to live with David, knowing how angry he was and the fact that he told her to stay away from him. He did not want her to cook for him, and she felt that if he was too angry to eat with her, he might hurt her. He also said he didn't want to talk with her, so she couldn't express her fears to him. Did he want her out of the house? She felt she would feel better if he simply cursed her out and told her to get out of the house, but living with him and not being able to communicate was going to seem too strange and unbearable for her.

CHAPTER 50

She could only eat a small bowl of soup for dinner. Her stomach was in knots. She wished that somehow David would reflect on everything she had said to him about her visit to LA and how she did not sleep with Greg, but she knew the photo of Greg kissing her breast overshadowed all reason. She had absolutely no definite way of proving to David that nothing had happened between them. She could only pray that he would realize she had never cheated on him during their marriage and that she never would. She had explained to him that when Greg advanced on her at the pool, she had pushed him away. She hoped he would reflect on how she explained her reactions to Greg that day.

After eating a bowl of soup, she went into the living room and turned on the television. The news was on, and she listened to reports of drive-by shootings and how the city had failed to clear away tall weeds in vacant land areas. By six thirty, David returned home. She had purposefully remained in the living room, to see if he would acknowledge her, but he did not. He merely hung his coat and hat in the closet, wiped his boots on the rug at the entrance to the living room, and walked past Maria and down the hall to the guest room, carrying his briefcase. He went into the room, closing the door behind him. Maria wondered how they could live under the same roof and not acknowledge each other, but she had to play by his rules. He owned their home. She could not order him to leave. It would hurt her to avoid him, but she didn't have a choice.

Several days went by, and Maria and David did not speak to each other, but Maria relaxed, realizing that David did not intend to harm her. She felt even better after she called Jonathan one evening and explained to him how someone had taken incriminating photos of her when she was on vacation in LA in October, and everything that followed. Jonathan felt outraged. He said that some jealous and evil person was trying to destroy the close bond she shared with his father and that he would talk with his father and advise him to reconsider the negative feelings. Maria couldn't thank Jonathan enough for his support.

Maria waited a week before calling Jonathan again. During that week, David did not exchange any words with her, and she nervously called Jonathan to find out what David said to him. Jonathan said that his father said he would think on the matter and would do so in silence. He said he had no desire to discuss the matter any further with her and that after a few weeks, he would let her know his decision. Maria told Jonathan she would call him again once his father decided to talk with her, and Jonathan said that would be fine.

During the weeks that followed, David and Maria lived in the home together in silence. It was very difficult for Maria to live that way, and she often thought about simply moving into an apartment, but she felt she had not done anything wrong, and if she moved out, David might divorce her.

CHAPTER 51

Finally, in early March, David decided to talk with Maria. When he came home from work at six thirty, he walked into the living room where she was stretched out on the sofa, watching television, and he asked her to please turn off the television. She turned it off.

"I've decided to leave the country," David said. Maria looked at him in shock. "I don't know what caused you to have a fling with that man in LA, but I do know that it's time for us to separate for a while. Perhaps we've just lost those special feelings that we once felt toward each other."

Maria sat up on the sofa and looked David straight in his eyes. "David, I've never lost the love I feel for you in my heart, and I never will," she said.

David bowed his head and stared at the floor for a long while. "Apparently, you had become bored with me, and perhaps with your life here in Sherwood Forest was the reason you went all the way to LA looking for some excitement."

"No, I—I merely went there to see how the artists were living. You know I've always admired them. I felt that they had it all. I hope you understand. I just wanted to know if their lives were any better than my own, and I realized that I have much more than they do because I've always had true love, David. They have money and drugs and sex, but very few of them have true love."

David was silent for a few moments and then said, "You were searching for excitement, Maria, and I guess you found it. There's no way you can excuse the way you felt. Maybe you decided that all that glitters ain't gold, but you were constantly with that man, that Greg Richmond, and I can't overlook how much time you spent with him." David paused for a moment. "And you can't shift the blame on the person who took photographs of you and Greg. You are to blame for your actions."

Maria slumped over on the sofa and softly cried.

"So, I'm going away for a while. I'm taking a year of sabbatical leave from the university, and I'm going to Europe. I want to visit Germany and tour the area where my parents once lived, and I want to visit Amsterdam, where they lived when they escaped Germany, and I'll visit Italy and Greece."

Maria wailed and sobbed very loudly, but David ignored her.

"I'm leaving in two weeks. While I'm gone, you can decide if you want to live with me, faithfully, as my wife, or if you wish to get a divorce. You can decide. I will accept your decision."

"David, please don't go," Maria wept.

"Maria, it is too late to plead with me. You should have thought more seriously about what you were doing when you took those trips to LA. I will leave for Europe in two weeks. I've talked with Jonathan and told him. I instructed him to keep in close contact with you. I will not contact you while I'm away, and I don't want you contacting me."

"How am I supposed to live without you?" Maria asked.

"You know damn well how to live without me," David scornfully replied, feeling the deep pains of knowing Maria had been unfaithful toward him.

She trembled, not knowing what to say.

"You knew how to deceive me about those trips you took, and a blind person could see how you were fooling around with another man." David stood up. "I'll continue to pay the mortgage, but you will have to pay the utility bills if you want electricity, water, and heat. There is a list of companies that can do repair work, with their telephone numbers, in the top drawer on my desk in the study."

"Will you write me?" Maria asked, feeling hopeful.

"No," David replied. "I will write in a journal, but I won't write you. End of discussion. I have nothing further to say to you." David walked out of the room. Maria continued to sit on the sofa, holding her head in the palms of her hands. She felt that everything in her beautiful life had turned dark and uncertain, and her future seemed so obscure that her mind went blank.

CHAPTER 52

The next day at work, Maria avoided small talk with everyone in the admissions office, and she continued to avoid talking with her coworkers the following week. Finally, Cynthia approached her and told her they needed to have lunch together because she was concerned about the gloomy feelings Maria was displaying. They went to a Greek restaurant on campus and were quickly waited on.

"So, what in the world is going on with you?" Cynthia demanded, looking at Maria sternly. "You've been walking around the office looking like a zombie."

Maria felt comatose. David would depart for Europe that weekend, and he had not expressed any kind words toward her. She was in a deathlike state.

"David is leaving me," Maria said, and Cynthia nearly spilled the water she was drinking. "He's taken a sabbatical, and he's going to spend a year in Europe."

The waitress walked up and set down an iced tea for Maria and one for Cynthia and then rushed away.

Cynthia stared at Maria in shock. "You mean he's still feuding with you about your vacations in California?" Cynthia asked as she stirred sugar into her tea.

"Feuding?" Maria said mockingly. "He's leaving."

"Honestly," Cynthia hissed, "it's unbelievable how vindictive he's become. I mean, he hasn't spoken to you in months. You two haven't slept together, and now he's leaving for Europe?"

"Yes, he's leaving me. He's taking a flight to New York on Saturday morning, and from there, he's heading to Germany."

"Why would he want to go to Germany?"

"So, he can see where his parents once lived and other relatives as well. He wants to get in touch with his roots. This is a trip he has been thinking about for many years, and I guess now he feels he has to go there and fulfill his longing to know about the past."

"And just leave your life in shambles," Cynthia remarked.

"That's his plan. He hasn't forgiven me for the foolish things I've done."

The waitress walked up and set down Cynthia's large Greek salad, and a spinach pie for Maria.

"Can I get you anything else?" the waitress asked.

"No, thank you," Maria replied, and the waitress walked to another table. She and Cynthia began eating.

"Lord, you know what I think?" Cynthia asked, looking a bit perplexed. Maria merely gazed at her in silence. "I think David really flipped out when he discovered you were seeing Greg Richmond. I mean, if you had met with John Doe, I think he would have gotten over it a lot faster."

Maria remained silent. She was thinking about how she would feel, living alone in such a big house. She knew she would be terribly frightened, and she couldn't imagine David leaving her all alone, not for an entire year.

"I believe he wants to see if I'll run back to Greg," Maria finally said.

"Or if not to Greg, to someone," Cynthia injected. "He's setting a trap for you. He knows you wouldn't like living alone."

"You're right, but I'm going to make it. I'm going to remain in my home, and I'll have Lenny to help me if I face any problems, such as minor repairs. We have an excellent alarm system, and that makes me feel good."

"Lenny is the guy who cares for your lawns, right?"

"Right. I've known him since we worked at Motown together in the sixties."

"Yes, I know. I remember you told me he used to chauffeur the Gordy family and Stevie Wonder. He sounds like a good guy, and I know you said he had been married for many years and that he has two children."

"That's right. His wife passed away nearly two years ago. I felt very sorry for him because he and his wife had been together for many years, but he's doing good. He never fails to cut my grass."

"It's good you have a friend like that."

After lunch, Maria and Cynthia returned to work, and Maria felt as if a load of worry and doubt had been lifted from her shoulders by engaging in conversation with a good friend. Cynthia promised Maria that they would get together and go bike riding in Kensington Park, and they could play tennis together, and she would call her at least twice during the week. Maria appreciated the support that Cynthia was offering.

CHAPTER 53

That Saturday morning, Maria heard the alarm clock going off at seven in David's room. She jumped out of bed, hoping she could hug him before his departure. He had telephoned a neighbor and asked for a ride to the airport, and the neighbor agreed. He would pick David up at eight o'clock. David had packed two suitcases, and he was fully dressed and ready to leave by eight. Maria raced down the hall toward him, but he merely rushed out the front door and walked to his neighbor's car that was parked in his driveway. Maria stood at the picture window and watched David as he left for the airport, and tears streamed down her face. She never once imagined David leaving her. She felt like a criminal who was being punished for a terrible crime. She sat on the sofa for a long while and cried. After breakfast, she began searching through her CDs, trying to find one that would express her profound love for David, and she found Jerry Butler's CD that had his hit song on it, "For Your Precious Love." She played the CD in the den, listening carefully to the words, as her mind began drifting.

She felt she had been foolish for getting in touch with Greg Richmond when she was in California and wondered why she had allowed her fascination with him to ruin her marriage. She knew that she deeply loved David, and she regretted how she had hurt him. Even more than that, she dreaded how he was leaving her. She knew that he had always been very loyal to her. Soon, she heard Jerry Butler singing "He Will Break Your Heart," and she listened very carefully to the words because Greg did not measure up in any way to the kind of genuine love that David offered her. Jerry Butler was singing these words:

He don't love you
like I love you.
If he did
he wouldn't break your heart.
He don't love you
like I love you.
He's trying to tear us apart.
Fare thee well, I know you're leaving …

When the song ended, Maria fully realized that Greg would never love her the way that David did, and she felt very disloyal to David by the way she had taken off to California, chasing a foolish dream. She couldn't blame David for putting distance between them, but she knew she would have to pray day and night to ask God to help her get through their separation. She knew the only man she loved was David.

As the weeks sailed by, Lenny was at Maria's home, cutting the grass, and in mid-May, he rang her doorbell one Saturday morning. She answered the door and invited him in. She had eaten breakfast and was in the kitchen drinking coffee. Lenny said that he had coffee before he left his home, but he wanted to talk with her for a few minutes. They sat at the kitchen table.

"I haven't seen David," Lenny said.

"He's in Europe," Maria replied with a deadly stare on her face.

"Europe?" Lenny exclaimed. "What's he doing over there?"

"Discovering his roots," Maria remarked as she sipped her coffee.

"What? You mean he went to Germany, where so many Jews were tortured and killed?"

Maria began crying and set down her coffee cup. Lenny walked over to her and took her by the arm.

"Come on, let's go into the living room and sit down so we can talk, and I'll tell you what you can do," Lenny said, holding Maria by the arm. They walked into the living room and sat on the sofa. Lenny tenderly kissed her. "You know you can depend on me," he said, "and if you feel lonely at night, just call me, and I'll come over."

Maria dried her eyes.

"Lenny, you know I can't do anything like that," she scolded him. "David is furious at me for traveling to California and visiting Greg Richmond; that's why he's left me. Do you think I'd have any desire to cause him to feel even more animosity toward me?"

"No, I know you wouldn't want to make him any angrier than he already is, but if you need any help around the house, just let me know."

"Thanks, Lenny."

CHAPTER 54

Lenny relaxed on the sofa.

"Damn, you went all the way to LA and met with Greg?" Lenny could hardly believe how much interest Maria had in Greg.

"I took a vacation and went to LA and met with a few of my friends who worked at Motown. You probably remember Sylvia Brown, Denise Hardin, and Sandra Evans."

"Yeah, sure I do. Sylvia and Denise worked in publicity, and Sandra was in accounting."

"I met with them for lunch and shopping, but Greg took me to his gorgeous home that was on a hill overlooking a valley, and he showed me the beautiful mansions that Berry, Smokey, Diana, and the Jacksons owned."

"I used to visit them," Lenny said. "I know how fabulous those houses are. So, how did David find out about you and Greg?"

"Some character was spying on me and took photos of me and Greg and showed them to David."

Lenny laughed. "David probably paid someone to take those pictures," Lenny said. "I don't think he ever felt comfortable about the fact that you knew so many people at Motown. I've always felt that he was probably pretty sneaky. His family may have told him that they felt he couldn't trust you."

Maria sighed deeply. "I don't know who took those pictures. David wouldn't tell me, but they made me so angry, I tore them up and threw them away."

"So, how did you like spending time with Greg?"

"I've always looked upon him as a good friend, Lenny. He has a lot of fans in Los Angeles."

Lenny laughed again. "You mean, he has a lot of women. I told you that's how those entertainers live."

"Yes, well, he was just a friend."

"I know, but David doesn't know that, and while he's in Europe, don't think he's not going to notice the women over there."

Maria looked deeply reflective for a few moments. "I've thought about that. He might end up divorcing me."

"Or he might stay over there."

Maria shivered. "It's all my fault," she said, as tears fell down her cheeks. "I pushed him away, all because of the way I was venturing out to see the other side of Motown, and the way the artists were living after the company had been sold."

"And how Greg was doing," Lenny added.

Maria dried her eyes. "David might never forgive me," she confessed.

"Well, at least he didn't throw you out; he could have."

"He told me to think about how I care to live; if I want to be a faithful wife to him. I've always been faithful to him."

"He has his doubts," Lenny stated. "Those photos really sent him over the edge."

Maria sighed. "I have no idea who followed me when I was in LA. I never saw anyone taking any photos of me and Greg, but they were too close for comfort."

"They were probably staying in the same hotel you were in," Lenny suggested.

"They may have been, but whoever took those photos wanted to make David upset with me. It was probably one of his friends who had advised him not to marry an African American woman."

"I felt sooner or later you'd have to face the kinds of prejudices people feel toward us. It's not right, but there's no way you can get around it. There are people who feel that blacks are inferior and should be kept at the bottom in life."

"I get sick of that kind of thinking," Maria snapped. She felt all people were the same. "I love Maya Angelou for saying 'And, still I rise.'"

"I like that saying also," Lenny said. "Well, you don't know how David feels deep down inside. He was probably so hurt, he needed to get away for a while. He's the only one who knows what he really wants. He has to decide if he wants to hold on to you or let go. If he decides to let go, I am here for you."

CHAPTER 55

"Lenny," Maria said, "my heart belongs to David. I just have to keep being faithful to him, even though he's far away, because he has been my soulmate all these years. We became close friends when he noticed me all alone on Wayne State's campus."

"I understand," Lenny replied. "Shirley came here from Georgia, and she didn't know people, so when our friends introduced us, we decided to stay together. We were separated a couple of times, but we made up and got back together. Life is a journey," Lenny added, "and you're always striving to get through it the best you can. A lot of things hurt and disappoint us, but God steps in and gives us the willpower to continue on."

"That is so true," Maria agreed, not knowing how David felt. She wondered if he'd find happiness in another part of the world and decide to remain there; she wasn't certain, and the feelings ripped through her body.

"Well, I have to get back to work," Lenny said as he stood up to leave. "You can call me at any time. I'm always busy working until six in the evening, but you can reach me any time after that."

"Okay, thanks, Lenny."

Lenny departed.

Maria felt that one of the ways she could endure living alone would be to continue with her writing. She began thinking about writing a novel entitled *The Forbidden Summer*. She could write about how a married woman felt bored and restless after her son, an only child, married and left home, and how an old friend, a musician, invited her into his world. She would explain how meeting with this man destroyed her marriage. She knew she had to get to a store and buy a few spiral notebooks so she could begin writing her story. She enjoyed handwriting her stories before typing them on her laptop. She could think more clearly while writing than while typing.

As the weeks passed, Maria had written over five hundred pages in her novel. Every time she wrote a novel, she felt that her ideas became clearer and more profound. Once she finished *The Forbidden Summer*, she was going to submit it to a publisher. For the first time in her life, she felt confident enough about a story to send it to a publisher.

Jonathan had called her twice over the past two months as she spent her time at home after work, writing her novel. He told her that David was doing fine and that he was renting an apartment in Frankfurt, Germany, where he would be for six months. He had already walked through the neighborhood where his parents once lived, taking photographs of everything of importance to him in Frankfurt. He would also visit other cities in Germany, and then he would tour Italy and Greece for a couple of months. After that, he would settle into Amsterdam, where his parents once lived when they escaped Germany. Jonathan said he was expected back at the university by the first of April. Maria thanked Jonathan for his information and told him to talk with his father at least once a week and to always let him know that she loved him. Jonathan said he would do that and wished his mother good luck with her novel.

Soon, Maria began typing her novel on her laptop. She knew it would take her a couple of months to type her story, and then she was going to submit it to a top-ranking publisher and hope for the best. She played Motown's music as she labored to complete her novel. Her love for Motown would endure forever.

CHAPTER 56

David stood at the window inside his apartment in Frankfurt. He had a one-bedroom apartment on the third floor of a four-story apartment building, with a view of the Main River. He loved watching ships and yachts as they sailed by and noticing the people who were leaving his apartment building, heading for work. He was located near the downtown area and had spent several days dining out and reading whatever publications he could find that were written in English.

It was near the end of May, and he had been to Sachsenhausen, south of the Main River, and had toured many fine museums in the area. He especially enjoyed the German Film Museum, which helped to enlighten him about the German filmmaking industry and shed light on the subtleties of everyday life in Germany. He had also discovered a small museum that contained very graphic photographs of the Holocaust, which were painful for him to view, but he knew he would have to embrace reminders of such a horrific period. He could only sigh and think, *Thank God it's over,* but could only wonder if the forces of evil would ever arise again to such a frightful state; he prayed they would not.

He ate a late breakfast and went for a stroll along the river close to noon. He noticed a young woman sitting alone on a bench, reading a newspaper. She was quite attractive—tall, slender, well-built, with a smooth complexion and beautiful, thick, black hair that was swept to one side of her face. He guessed by her dark hair and eyes that she was also Jewish.

He walked up to her and asked, "Mind if I sit next to you?"

"Not at all." She smiled, and his heart melted at the sight of her beautiful smile. He longed for one-on-one contact with someone. He noticed that she was reading the *Wall Street Journal*.

He sat down. "Is that paper written in English?" he asked.

"Yes. I buy it at a bookstore near the Financial District."

"Do you work in finance?"

"Yes, I'm an investment banker from Chicago. I'm here on business."

"I'm a professor at Wayne State University in Detroit. I'm here touring Germany while on sabbatical. I'm David Silverman." He extended his hand toward her. She immediately grasped his hand and shook it, anxious to meet an American.

"I'm Amelia Fineberg. I'm staying at the Moxy in Ostend. I'll be here for three weeks."

"I have an apartment that's a few blocks from here. I'll be here until the end of August, and then I plan to tour Italy and Greece."

"And are you traveling alone?"

"Yes. I'm separated from my wife."

"I see," Amelia replied. "I'm divorced. I'm forty-seven, and my husband left me for a woman half my age. I'm beginning to think of it as a hobby—you know, older men chasing after younger women."

David sighed. "I understand. Life is complicated."

Amelia folded her newspaper and tucked it into her purse. "So, do you think that's fair? For men to give up their trusted mate and companion for some stranger?"

"No, I simply feel that people get to a point in life that they don't know what they want."

"Is that how you feel?"

"No. I have always loved my wife, but she became attracted to someone else."

Amelia felt that was just perfect. She could possibly enjoy David's company without worrying about him being married. It didn't seem as if he'd be married for very much longer. He was so disgusted with his wife, he had left the country.

"You should join me for lunch at three. You can take a cab to the Moxy, and I'll meet you at the front entrance. We can walk a few blocks to the Heidel Café and have lunch. There are many cafés and boutiques in the area, and you'd enjoy it."

"Certainly, we can do that. I'll meet you at three."

David stood and said goodbye and walked back to his apartment, feeling good inside. It was wonderful meeting Amelia, and it helped him to relax, knowing there was someone from his country with whom he could converse. He had grown weary of speaking a few short sentences in German to total strangers. He kept his small German-language book with him at all times.

CHAPTER 57

At three o'clock, he met Amelia, and they walked to the Heidel Café. Ostend was a very modern and pleasant section of Frankfurt that was filled with many cafés and small, interesting shops. In a short while, they were seated in the café and ordered lunch. Amelia order sausage and sauerkraut, and David ordered a baked chicken breast in cream sauce, with potatoes and brussels sprouts. They had red wine to drink.

Soon, they began eating and continued to discuss how Germany had grown immeasurably over the past several decades, leading the world in manufacturing and finance. Amelia had visited several areas of the city and felt comfortable in Frankfurt. She wouldn't mind returning to the city next year for a visit. David missed Maria something awful and wished they had never gotten into an argument, but he wondered if it was possible to live with one mate for your entire life and not face some major conflict. He doubted very seriously if it was possible to avoid serious disagreements, but he never felt he'd find himself leaving his home and traveling as far as Europe. He actually yearned to be back home. He was deep in thought as Amelia rattled on about all the culture and history surrounding them in Germany.

"You're so quiet," she said as the waiter set down their second round of drinks.

David put forth a small smile. How could he possibly hide from any woman how much he loved his wife?

"Just thinking about the language," he said, and Amelia laughed.

"I listened to several CDs that helped me to learn how to pronounce words in German," she said. "It's better to hear someone speaking the language than to merely try to remember words that are written phonetically."

"I wish I had given the language barrier better consideration before I left home," David replied.

"I bet you left in the heat of passion, simply thinking how wonderful it would be to put distance between you and your wife."

"Yes, that is so true; that's how it happened."

"So, it was your first time separating from her."

"Yes."

"Do you regret it?"

David had to think hard for several moments. "I feel the separation was inevitable."

"Meaning that things had been rocky for quite some time."

"Actually, I never knew about the other guy; it was a shock when I found out."

"You mean she confessed that she was in love with someone else?"

David was thinking more clearly for the first time in a long while since he found out about Greg Richmond. "No, she never confessed that she was in love with someone else."

Amelia felt like throwing her steak knife into the wall. She liked David a great deal and could almost feel him next to her in her bed. What the hell was wrong with his stupid wife? Why didn't she simply admit she had fallen in love with someone and wanted a divorce?

CHAPTER 58

A melia silently drew in a breath. "So, how did you find out that she had been seeing someone?"

David hesitated. He did not want to admit that a close friend of his took photographs of Maria with another man, because that would cause Amelia to feel that he was a very jealous and paranoid person. He had to answer very carefully. "Someone told me about their affair," he said.

Amelia smiled pleasantly, thinking, *Well, good; someone told him that his wife was a rat.* "And you argued and fought, and then you decided it was best to put distance between the two of you."

"Yes, exactly."

Amelia was quiet for a long while as they sipped wine. She felt hot all over. David was like a ripe plum that was ready to be picked. She hadn't had sex in over a year, and finally she had met someone she was certain needed good loving just as much as she did. Her eyes began to sparkle. "Have you heard about the Red Room?" she asked.

David's hands began to tremble, and a dread swept over him as Amelia stared at his hands. He felt embarrassed. *Calm down,* he kept telling himself. "No, I haven't," he managed to reply.

"It's a red-hot nightclub," Amelia said. "It's nothing bad and definitely nothing you would regret. You and I both need to dance and laugh and make ourselves feel good. You'd love it," she assured him.

"It … sounds like a fun place," he said, trying to remember the last time he'd gone dancing. Maybe this trip was teaching him how to relax and enjoy life, and maybe he had been too hard on Maria. Perhaps he had always expected her to be perfect, and no one was perfect. He needed to learn to relax and enjoy life and not take himself too seriously.

"We should go to the Red Room this Friday," Amelia said. "Come here to my hotel at nine thirty. I'll meet you in the lobby, and I can drive us to the club. I have a rental."

"Okay, I'll do that. I haven't been dancing in quite a few years, and I look forward to it. I enjoy good music."

"Do you have children?"

"I have a son who is married and has three kids. He and his wife live in Hawaii."

"So, you've seen your son dancing. I don't have children, but I'm sure you took your son to dances."

"True. I've simply spent a lot of time traveling with my students in my history classes, and I haven't spent much time on a dance floor."

"But once you hear all that good music, you won't have a problem," Amelia said as they finished their second glass of wine.

David laughed. "I'm sure you're right."

Later that evening, David was feeling intrigued by Amelia. She was quite attractive, and he enjoyed her company. He was beginning to understand how Maria must have felt once she met Greg Richmond. No doubt, she had felt very intrigued also. He decided he had nothing to worry about by being in Amelia's company. She would be in Frankfurt for only a short while, and there wouldn't be any harm in enjoying her company for a few days.

CHAPTER 59

That Friday, Amelia met David in the lobby of her hotel and drove them to the Red Room in her rented Lexus SUV. The club was only a mile away, on a back street in the downtown area; she stopped behind three cars that were waiting for a valet. Soon, a valet attendant approached and gave Amelia a parking ticket, and she and David exited the vehicle and went inside the club. The club was quite spacious and crowded with people in their twenties, thirties, and forties. David was much older, but he knew that in this crowded club with its red lights, no one would care about his age.

He and Amelia found a table near the center of the club and got seated. A young waitress in black shorts and a black halter top took their drink order. They both ordered cognac, straight up. After their drinks arrived, they took a few swallows and then went out on the dance floor. They were eager to mix with the crowd and all that energy. Amelia was impressed with the way David danced so smoothly to the beat of the music, and she kept him out on the dance floor for nearly a half hour. He was glad to return to their table and drink and chat for a good while. They ordered a second round, and this time when they went out on the dance floor, they stayed a bit longer. Amelia was able to dance a slow number with David and rub her body against him. The feeling of her warm, soft body sent sensations all through him. He had not made love in several months, and he felt himself swelling and longing to have sex. Before he and Amelia left the club at one o'clock in the morning, he was burning with desire to make love. Amelia drove straight to the Moxy;

they took the elevator to the tenth floor and were soon inside her room. They kissed for a long while before Amelia told David to make himself comfortable on the sofa while she changed into something comfortable.

While Amelia was in her room changing into a negligee, David had a sudden flashback. He could see Maria on the floor, grabbing on to his leg and crying and pleading to him, explaining to him that she did not sleep with Greg Richmond. His heart began beating like thunder. He remembered Maria exclaiming that nothing had happened between her and Greg. Amelia walked up to him, wearing a short, see-through lavender gown that exposed her luscious breasts and beautiful form, but only terror rushed through him when he realized that he had failed to listen to Maria.

"I have to go!" David said in a loud voice, as if lightning had struck him. He realized he had walked out on his wife and had left her home alone, and he had no idea how she was doing. Someone could break in and kill her, and how would he feel being far away from home on another continent, in some woman's hotel room? He would feel like killing himself.

"What's wrong?" Amelia asked.

"I'm sorry, but I must go," David nervously replied, his hands trembling. "I've never slept with any woman other than my wife, and I'm not about to do so now."

David rushed to the door and let himself out. Amelia shook her head in disgust. Why did she have to pick such a lemon? Here she was, dressed in her most expensive negligee, and the one man she felt more attracted to than any other in recent years had fled out the door. She fell down on her sofa and hoped she'd never see that jerk again.

David took a cab to his apartment, and once inside, he quickly undressed and crawled into bed. He knew he wasn't ready to live like a single man. He loved being married to his wife. He didn't expect Amelia to understand how he felt. She was happy to have divorced her husband, and he couldn't blame her for wanting to start over, except she couldn't do so with him.

CHAPTER 60

The next morning, David woke up at eleven o'clock and immediately got into the shower. He was greatly relieved that he had escaped Amelia and had not broken his marital vows. He believed in his heart that Maria had not broken her vows either but that she had entertained thoughts about the rich and the famous and had been anxious to find out how they lived. Greg Richmond was available and ready to take her into his world, but she refused to follow him. All the same, he knew Maria needed to learn how to appreciate what she had in life. She had true love, and they had a solid bond. He had even come to realize just how fortunate they were. A person could travel the world and yet not find a special person like his wife with whom he shared an intimate union.

As he stepped out of the shower, his phone began ringing. He grabbed a towel, wrapped it around him, and rushed to the phone. "Hello."

"Hi, Dad. How are you?"

"I'm fine, Jonathan. I went to a nightclub last night with a group of Americans who live in my building, and it was something else, trying to dance with a bunch of young people."

Jonathan laughed. "I know that was a funny sight. Everything's fine here at home. The children are more active than ever. I talked with Mother yesterday, and she's doing good. She just misses you a great deal."

"I miss her too, but we needed some time to ourselves so that we could come to appreciate how we feel about our marriage."

"I'm sure you feel positive," Jonathan said.

"Yes, of course," David quickly replied, "but I believe your mother felt she had missed out on a lot of fun and enjoyment after she left Motown and married me."

"Whoa!" Jonathan exclaimed. "Then I wouldn't be here."

David laughed. "Of course you would be here, but I felt Maria needed time alone so she could come to appreciate the life she has with me. It seems as if she had become bored."

"I don't think she felt bored," Jonathan countered, "just curious about the people in LA."

"Yes, well, it's very nice here in Frankfurt."

"Which means?"

"Which means I enjoy it a great deal."

"I hope you're not considering staying there."

"No, so far, I'm just enjoying all the sights, taking photos, and keeping a journal. I'll have a lot to share with my students once I return next year."

"We miss you," Jonathan said.

"I miss you too, but this is one wonderful adventure for me to experience the city where my parents grew up and where their families lived. I have visited the historic district where they once lived, and I will tour Berlin in a few days. Everything is going real fine. So, what has your mother been doing?"

"She's busy writing a novel. Something about how a housewife got bored with being at home all the time, and she took a three-week vacation to LA and reunited with an old lover."

David felt his ears burning. "An old lover?"

"You know how Mother writes fiction."

David could barely calm down. "Yes, I know, but isn't it interesting that she's chosen to write about vacationing in LA?"

"Well, what if she wrote that this housewife went to Europe instead?"

"Okay, enough said. You are really criticizing both me and your mother, but I feel that we needed time to ourselves. I'm sure your mother learned a lot when she was in LA, and I'm enjoying being here in Germany and discovering my roots. It's a beautiful and yet painful experience. I visited a Holocaust museum and viewed hundreds of photographs of all the brutal persecutions that were carried out here under Hitler's regime."

"We've always known about that," Jonathan lamented.

"Yes, but I had never seen photographs like the ones I saw in that museum."

"So, we can be thankful that Hitler and his regime were defeated."

"And pray that such hatred never arises again." They were silent for a while, then David added, "I'm glad you called me. I will be traveling quite a bit, but I will always call you and let you know where I'm staying."

"Okay. I love you, Dad."

"I love you too."

They said goodbye and hung up. David dried off, dressed, and went to a nearby restaurant to have lunch.

CHAPTER 61

Maria had spent most of the summer riding her bike through Kensington Park, along with Cynthia, who loved the great outdoors just as much as she did. They had also played several games of tennis in Palmer Park, not far from their neighborhood, and Cynthia had won four of the six games they played. Maria disliked how strenuous the tennis games were, but she didn't complain because she knew how much Cynthia enjoyed beating her. Maria could ride her bike and think about David and wonder how he was getting along in Europe. On the tennis court, there was no time for contemplation, only fast action, which she was never prepared for, and Cynthia constantly slammed balls by her.

Maria was glad that she had finished her novel, *The Forbidden Summer*, and had sent it to the North Chest Publishing Company in Philadelphia, Pennsylvania. They published books dealing with adventure, sports, travel, hobbies and crafts, biographies and autobiographies, and historic and contemporary romance stories. She mailed her novel to them in late June, and it was now near the end of July and she had not heard from them. She feared that a rejection letter was on its way, but as long as her husband returned home safely by next spring, that was all that mattered to her. She felt she might never become an author, but she was a married woman, and she greatly desired to save her marriage. She dreaded that David had seen those photos of her and Greg, and she felt he may have lost faith in her. He was visiting quite a few cities in Europe, and being the kind of pleasant and friendly person he was, he could easily attract a nice lady. Every day that she had faced since David's departure had been filled with dread.

Lenny always showed up at her home every two weeks to cut her grass, but she would never invite him in. She would only pay him and tell him she was busy working on a novel and did not have time to converse with him. He said he understood. He knew she didn't care to get involved with him, and he had started dating a nurse who had helped his wife when she was ill. He was making good progress in building a relationship with her. She had been divorced from an abusive husband for five years and was glad to have Lenny in her life.

During the second week in August, Maria received a letter from the North Chest Publishing Company which stated her novel, *The Forbidden Summer*, had been accepted for publication. She was given the name and telephone number of a publishing coordinator and was told to contact her in order to discuss a publishing agreement. Maria was so thrilled, she called all of her friends and her son and told them the good news. They were all very happy for her, knowing that since she began taking English classes at Wayne State in the 1970s, she had hoped to someday become an author, and now, after more than thirty years, she had finally achieved her goal. Jonathan was especially happy for her, as he had witnessed how she had labored for many hours and years in her bedroom, writing stories that merely landed in a storage box. He told her that he would telephone his father in Berlin and let him know the good news.

Maria wished David would talk with her. She longed to express to him what it meant to her to have her first book published, but she knew that when David set down a rule, he would never break it. He told her he would absolutely not communicate with her until he returned home in the spring. But she knew Jonathan would convey her excitement and delight to him.

During the following months, Maria worked diligently with the publishing coordinator in editing her novel. It was very tedious work over the internet, but Maria loved every moment of it. Her first book was in the making, and it was as exciting as being pregnant and doing everything possible to bring a healthy baby into the world. Every month, she labored hard in working with the publishing coordinator to perfect her writing.

CHAPTER 62

David had enjoyed many sights in Berlin. He stayed in a hotel in Friedrichshain in Berlin's artsy hub, where he visited several museums. He drove his rental car over the Oberbaum Bridge, a checkpoint between West and East Germany, several times and talked with the local artists and musicians who performed under the bridge's concave.

One evening, a group of American artists invited him to the Berghain techno club, which could accommodate fifteen hundred people. It was the largest nightclub David had ever attended in his life, and it was fascinating for him to watch all the different people in the club.

He also went with the artists to Volkspark in Friedrichshain for a barbecue. The park was the oldest one in Berlin, and was adorned with sculptures, monuments, and fountains.

David thoroughly enjoyed his month's stay in Berlin before he took a flight to Rome, Italy. He spent a month in Italy and a month in Greece, touring both countries with tour groups. It was his second time in Italy and Greece since his senior year in college. He remembered many of the coliseums, temples, and theaters in Rome, and he loved the countryside, where there were many vineyards.

In Greece, he enjoyed the high hills overlooking the Aegean and Ionian seas. He stayed in a hotel in Athens and met a Greek family from the United States who invited him to travel with them to several Greek islands, where they enjoyed four days of festivities.

In Athens, David toured museums that displayed great art and historical events. He also enjoyed a large section of the historical museum that was dedicated to Greek philosophers.

Most of all, he loved the warm and friendly people in Greece and dining with them in quaint cafés and restaurants. Greece was a great agricultural country, and the wine and the food were the very best. He also enjoyed the small shops where he bought expensive leather products.

Soon, he settled into Amsterdam in Grachtengordel in the canal zone, where he stayed at the Hotel Goldmarie. One afternoon, he toured the Anne Frank House, a museum based on the life of a young Jewish girl who hid in her home from the Nazis. It deeply touched David's heart to think how this young girl managed to cling to a few months of life before being discovered by the Nazis. His subconscious mind caused him to worry about Maria and how she was doing, living alone at home. He had intended to punish her for her foolish behavior, yet in many ways he felt as if he had been punishing himself. He couldn't help worrying about her.

He didn't know exactly where in Amsterdam his parents had lived after they escaped Hitler, but he was glad to be there and to imagine the freedom they must have enjoyed for a while before departing for America. Amsterdam was filled with many old buildings and embraced an Old World atmosphere, although there were modern sections of the city here and there. It was a port city on the edge of the Netherlands by the North Sea, and David enjoyed cruising in boats along canals and dining in the canal area. One evening, an American doctor who was staying in his hotel invited him to dinner with him and his wife at the Librije Zusje, Amsterdam's Waldorf Astoria Hotel. They enjoyed a beautiful evening together in an exclusive diner.

David loved the way the chefs in Amsterdam prepared duck in many different tantalizing ways that were tender and seasoned with different spices and sometimes yogurt. One of his favorite meals was scallops with ginger zing, and artichokes and shiitake mushrooms.

One evening, David met an American musician while they were both viewing art in the world-famous Van Gogh Museum. The musician, who introduced himself to David as Jack, was on tour with his band, and in a couple of days, they would be leaving for the UK. He told David that after they finished viewing the art in the museum, he could show him a district in the city where women stood in front of the windows at their apartments and advertised their bodies for sex. David found himself blushing and speechless. Jack asked him if his wife was staying with him at the hotel, and he responded no and that a drive through this district he mentioned was all that was necessary. The man agreed with him.

An hour later, before dark, Jack drove through a seedy neighborhood where the women stood skimpily dressed, exposing their bodies. David closed his eyes and shook his head in disbelief, and Jack laughed.

"So, you wouldn't like one of those ladies?" Jack asked, laughing.

"No, not at all," David replied.

"If you're afraid of diseases, just wear a condom."

"No, I'm married. I don't sleep around."

Jack got an eyeful. A few women truly aroused his urges. He would visit at least two of them before the night ended.

He quickly drove David back to the Goldmarie Hotel, and they wished each other well and said good night. Once David was back in his room, he quickly undressed and plunged himself under a blanket as if he were trying to shut out the entire world.

CHAPTER 63

The weeks continued on as David toured Amsterdam and enjoyed cruises. Soon, it was December, and people were putting up lights and getting in the Christmas spirit. David felt extremely homesick and wished he was at home with Maria. He talked with Jonathan twice before Christmas and found out that Maria would be spending Christmas at his home in Honolulu. David told him to let her know that he missed her very much; it was the first time that he had admitted how much he missed her.

On Christmas Day, David attended a dinner party at his hotel and enjoyed a lavish meal with the guests. They were entertained by a children's and adults' choir until nine o'clock before everyone departed to their rooms. David was happy the day was over. It was the first time in decades that he had spent Christmas alone without his family, and he was anxious to return home.

Once Maria returned home from Hawaii, she retrieved all the mail from her mailbox and went inside her home. She hung up her coat, sat down on the sofa, and opened a stack of Christmas cards. All the cards were very beautiful, and everyone was wishing her and David a happy holiday season. Tears flooded Maria's eyes. She greatly missed David and wished he'd break his rule about not communicating with her until he returned from his travels. It was very painful living without him, and she was deeply sorry that she went chasing her dreams in California. She felt it wasn't worth the pain and agony she had to endure once David saw those photographs. She hated whoever the person was who was so eager to make her look bad to her husband. She cried for a long while and then dressed for bed. In no time, she was fast asleep.

In February, Maria received a telephone call from her publishing coordinator at North Chest Publishing, who informed Maria that her book would be released during the first week in March and that copies would be sent to bookstores throughout the country and made available online. Maria immediately called Jonathan and left him a voice mail, informing him about the good news. Maria also arranged book signings with several bookstores in southeastern Michigan.

Near the end of March, David returned home from his travels abroad. He drove home from the airport in a rental car and surprised Maria at eight o'clock in the evening when she was watching television. She heard the front door opening, and her heart began racing. She looked around and noticed David in a trench coat as he was setting down his luggage.

"David!" she cried and raced into his arms as tears streamed down her face.

He warmly hugged her and then tenderly kissed her.

"Thank God you're home!" she exclaimed.

"I'm glad to be home," he replied, feeling very exhausted.

"I'm so sorry we had that bitter fight. I will never travel alone ever again—I promise."

"Neither will I."

"I've always been faithful to you."

"And likewise," he said. "And I want this to be the last of our separations."

"I am so glad about that," Maria said. "I couldn't stand another day without you."

"That's all I need to hear. There is nothing in this world that I want more than you. Let's shower and get ready for bed."

Printed in the United States
By Bookmasters